The Accidental Adventures of Mariska Arisia

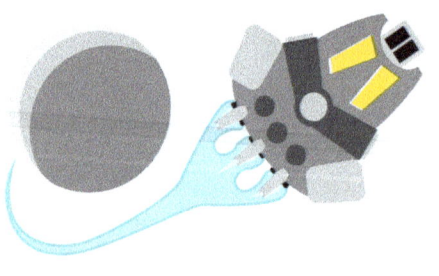

The Accidental Adventures of Mariska Arisia

By

Thomas J Bradley

17thousandpages.ca

17 Thousand Pages Publishing
Ottawa, Canada

17thousandpages.ca
feedback@17kp.ca

The text for this book is set in Avenir and Calendas Plus.

Paperback ISBN: 978-0-9936805-0-2
eBook ISBN: 978-0-9936805-1-9

To the quiet adventurer in all of us.

Contents

Part 1: Escaping Mycota

Part 2: Saving Minerallia

Space. Literally it means "nothing"—a vacuum between stars and planets. But by the same token, it means everything.

—*Captain Kathryn Janeway, Star Trek: Voyager*

The Old System

Ignirtoq

Mycota

Akycha

Ataksak

Vandia

The Accidental Adventures of Mariska Arisia

Part 1

Escaping Mycota

The *Stellar Hermes* had been blasting towards the outer rim of The First System, closing on its destination. The delivery should have been like every other—but it wasn't.

Bed of Basidiomycota

All Mariska wanted was a quick jaunt to the outer system with a few days of much needed solitude, just her and NAN-C, her sometimes too matronly computer. There had been too many interruptions recently: equipment failures, rogue gravity wells, and space pirates. She was beginning to worry about her pristine reputation.

The trip had been quite satisfying. Mariska had had time to review the schematics for the capacitive fluxeon ionizer she was waiting to buy; time to study some of the star maps for The Old System, which she hadn't yet travelled; and lots of alone time. Thankfully NAN-C didn't usually bother her like live beings. But NAN-C did sometimes talk too much—at least there was a mute button when Mariska needed some silence.

Mariska had been saving up for months to buy the new capacitive fluxeon ionizer. This high-paying courier job to the outer rim would earn her enough credits to purchase the much needed component for *Stellar Hermes*. She couldn't wait to install the new ionizer on her ship!

Of course, all this was immaterial when standing beside her recent wreck; it definitely wasn't going to improve her reputation, even if it was a respectable crash landing.

The whole nearly-plummeting-to-her-death event was fuzzy. Mariska couldn't remember very many distinct details. Everything had been humming along QX, when another ship flashed out of nowhere on her port side. The two ships swerved to avoid each other, careened down to the planet's surface under little control, where they finally smashed into the ground several kilometres apart. During the rapid descent, her mind was in shock, her adrenaline was pumping, and her vision was blurry. All of which lead to some muddy memories.

Mariska cursed the other captain under her breath.

Her disabled ship was a depressing site. *Stellar Hermes* was her home, even if it was a little ragtag. At least her vessel was mostly intact. There was a big dent on the front of the cockpit pod, just cosmetic; the belly was badly scratched and banged, nothing some good buffing and a paint job couldn't fix; and the thrust vectoring ailerons were misaligned, needing a few hours of pushing, pulling, and screwing to recalibrate. She patted herself on the back for not extending the landing gear because it would have been completely torn off.

But the old ionizer was a complete write-off. Without it her ship couldn't fly. Now she *really* needed the credits, not just for the new ionizer, but for all the rest of the repairs as well.

Overall it wasn't the worst that could have happened. With a few parts and some tender love, *Stellar Hermes* should fly—hopefully.

Most importantly her cargo didn't appear to be damaged.

Mariska stepped back inside her jalopy and tried radioing for help, but the subspace communications array must have been damaged. All she got was a few pathetic cackles of fuzz. So she clipped NAN-C's handheld terminal to her utility belt, stuffed the small cargo box and some supplies into her backpack, and slumped back outside. She looked up at her ship and sighed heavily. *Stellar Hermes* was her whole life—and it was a mess.

Mariska slammed a knob in frustration, closing the landing ramp. She took a deep breath, suppressed her emotions, and decided it was polite—and socially expected of her—to go find the other ship. Even if she had no interest in talking to another being—especially one that had caused this predicament.

There was also the remote possibility that the other ship was still space-worthy, and if so, Mariska was willing to pay for passage with some soul-sucking small talk.

Mariska walked a couple of metres away from her downed ship and NAN-C's orb component bobbed through the air with her, floating above her right shoulder. The orb was the size of a throwing ball, with protruding sensors scattered around the spherical surface, little extending antennae, flashing lights, and several hidden tools. The orb was one of three parts composing the Networked Autonomous Nanocomputer, Version C, system, with the other two pieces being *Stellar Hermes's* onboard computer, and the hand terminal on Mariska's utility belt. NAN-C was a multi-function, computer-robot hybrid device with a myriad of helpful functions— along with a motherly demeanour. Mariska often relied on NAN-C.

Mariska strained to see through the haze of humidity. She looked along the horizon of the mysterious planet, trying to find the direction of the other downed craft— but it was all just a blurry, wavy jumble of beiges, blues, and greens.

Turning her head towards the floating orb, Mariska spoke into the air: "NAN-C, what's the direction of the other ship?"

"During our dangerous landing, dear, I was not fully capable of determining the other vessel's approach vector. My preliminary calculations suggest that it is somewhere to the north-east of our current location," purred NAN-C's comforting tone.

Mariska couldn't see any signs of the other ship in that direction, but she trusted NAN-C.

"NAN-C, plant a marker here so we can find our way back," suggested Mariska.

"Of course, love," replied NAN-C.

Mariska, starting her quest, jumped down into the gorge *Stellar Hermes* had carved on its crash descent and headed towards a hillock on the other side of the ridge.

. . .

The planet didn't look unpleasant—but it *was* unpleasant because it wasn't part of Mariska's plan. She didn't get a chance to check what planet this was when she was trying to gain control of her spiralling vessel; she'd have to wait for the stars to be visible to plot her location. The planet was definitely remote, but hopefully not too far off route to delay her too much.

She just wanted to get this over with so she could repair her own ship and go back to her delivery.

The humidity was stifling. If she hadn't checked the atmospherics before exiting *Stellar Hermes* she wouldn't have believed this planet was hospitable. Her light grey tank top was a good choice in this heat, but being always prepared, Mariska made sure to pack her favourite cropped jacket as well.

The planet was lush and overgrown with green and brown leafy grasses, lichen, and lots of mushrooms. The flora was low, with no tall trees or even bushes, quite tundra-like.

Mariska's long legs made light work of strolling across the vegetation covered ground. She was mesmerized by the quantity and varieties of mushrooms and fungi. She noticed a clump of golden mushrooms with small spikes all over their caps; a single, stubby, red variety with white spots; and up ahead was a massive indigo mushroom with speckles. There were hundreds of plain-old white button mushrooms. Groupings of brown mushrooms huddled under rock outcroppings. Tall, thick, woody, sand-coloured fungi the height of her knee.

Everywhere she looked: mushrooms.

Mariska plucked a grey-stalked, aquamarine-capped fungus and inquisitively rolled it in her fingers. The mushroom was soft and spongy—and slimy. "NAN-C, are you able to identify these mushrooms?" asked Mariska.

"Yes, many of them. Yet, some of the fungi are foreign

to my databanks," replied the hovering NAN-C, cooing with love. "The one you're holding is a pixie's parasol. Just beside your left foot is a beaked earthstar, a wonderful variety of geastraceae with a stalked pore sac. We just passed a stinky squid. Its malodorous smell comes from the dark green slime covering its up-stretched arms. Just ahead on the right is a coral spring mycena—one of my favourites."

Sometimes it was confusing to be reminded that NAN-C was, in fact, a computer. *How could a computer have a favourite fungi?*

Mariska bent down to inspect a mushroom with reddish-orange scales hanging from the top. "That appears to be a pineapple bolete, but I cannot fully confirm. The colouring on the top does not match the varieties in my databanks. Maybe it is a planet specific variety," suggested NAN-C.

As Mariska continued walking north-east to find the other ship, NAN-C spouted descriptions of the myriad of visible fungi species: "We just passed a bundle of ebony cups, a saprobic fungus with fruit bodies shaped like small blackish cups. Up ahead is a bright yellow smooth chantrelle, a species of edible fungus. I can see a cluster of fairy fingers, or clavaria fragilis, to our left, a typical member of the clavarioid family. Your boot just crushed a small bleeding bonnet. Did you know they leak a dark reddish-purple sap when fresh? And over there is a quilted green russula with it's stunning pale green cap and patches of darker green; also edible, tasting nutty."

NAN-C's excitement for the fungi was invigorating.

Just ahead Mariska noticed a dark brown, speckled, ball-shaped fungi, about the size of her fist. Walking over, she kicked it with her work boot, exploding the puffball into a cloud of earthy smoke. The particles hung thickly in the air with the lack of wind, and slowly descended back to the ground.

"Be careful not to step on those gasterotheciums, honey, some of the spores from the puffball varieties are poisonous," cautioned NAN-C.

Mariska could have explored the mushroom field—or as NAN-C named it, The Bed of Basidiomycota—for hours. But she was hot: her hair was soaking with sweat and dripping down her forehead; the back of her shirt, behind her backpack, was so wet she could wring it out; even her knee-pits were steamy and damp.

And she was parched. She'd been so consumed with the fungi she had forgotten to drink.

Mariska plopped down to the ground for a rest, set her backpack beside her, and leaned against a boulder with a particularly tough looking, earth-toned bracket mushroom. Pulling out her water bottle, she gulped a large draft of water with a complete disregard for rationing.

I've been walking for over an hour and still no sign of the other vessel, thought Mariska. She was starting to regret leaving the comfort of her own ship, even if the Bed of Basidiomycota was intriguing to wander through.

"Any sign of the other crashed vessel, NAN-C?" asked Mariska.

"Nothing conclusive, though I am picking up a faint sound in that direction," responded NAN-C. And adding a suggestion: "Up ahead the ground seems to slope steeply downwards; it is possible we cannot see the other vessel because it is below our line of sight."

"QX. Thanks."

Even though NAN-C was just a digital voice, Mariska didn't mind having someone to love her—even if it was a little smothering.

Mariska sat next to the rock for a few minutes, with NAN-C bobbing around inspecting the flora. Mariska tried pulling her sopping shirt away from her back, attempting to cool it, but it was futile without wind. She'd just have to deal with a soaking tank top.

She stood up. She realized her braid wasn't very effective, since half of the strands had fallen out. Mariska tried to fix her mop of burgundy hair, but with the humidity it would puff back out in a minute or two—not that she cared about how her hair looked.

Bending over to pick up her backpack, she peaked inside to confirm her cargo was still there. It was an unconscious action—she knew it was still nestled inside.

Mariska strapped on her backpack, wincing as it touched her dripping wet shirt, and continued towards the nearby slope.

· · ·

The slope wasn't too far ahead and she still couldn't see anything beyond it, likely due to the haze. Getting closer, Mariska could hear a faint sound of grinding, like an engine struggling to run.

She was getting a little nervous. Meeting new people was always nerve-racking. She started to worry about what she was going to say if she found the other pilot alive. Maybe she wouldn't have to speak and the other pilot would do all the talking.

Mariska reached the crest of the slope and looked down the steep slide. Immediately at the bottom was a wrecked starship—looking much worse off than hers.

With equal parts excitement and trepidation, Mariska started her slide down the slope. It was treacherous, her feet slipping as she carefully took step after step down the incline. Her foot landed on a slimy bunch of mushrooms and slid out from under her. Mariska lost her balance and fell hard on her left palm.

"Frak," cursed Mariska, looking at her skinned hand. Her palm was stinging profusely but she continued downwards.

Mariska was disappointed with the harm she was causing to all the interesting mushrooms on the slope, but her own safety was slightly more important.

Reaching the bottom, there was a burning smell, but thankfully nothing was on fire.

As she got closer to the downed craft, she realized how big it was. The ship was the size of a large mansion and bulky like a cargo freighter. It was destroyed yet she could still discern what it formerly looked like. It was very symmetrical and boxy, but not a rectangle, more like an octagonal prism if you could look at it end-wise. The main body of the vessel had buttresses that wrapped around, like ribs holding it together, many bent and dented from the crash. The aft had three large, protruding thrusters, and the bow was flat, with a large array of portholes, making it look really un-aerodynamic.

The vessel had dug a long, deep gorge, just like *Stellar Hermes*, and seemed to be resting on a mound of dirt out front, canted to the rear-starboard.

She suddenly realized what the sound was: the large landing ramp, opening towards her on the port site, was jammed under a big rock and was trying to close. It kept jolting up, making a grinding sound, then falling back down to repeat the process. The fact that the ramp was stuck *under* a rock was a little odd, but she didn't dwell on it.

She started to walk towards the freighter. Hopefully there were survivors, but from where she was standing, she couldn't see anybody. Mariska ambled towards the open hatch, climbed onto the rock, and started to peek inside. "Anybody there?" she called.

Mariska moved closer to the opening, knocked loudly on the side of the ship and shouted: "Anybody alive?"

She was about to go inside, but lost her footing. It was as though the ground had moved, causing her to topple hard onto the boulder.

A grumbling sound startled her.

The rock was moving.

And groaning—

Chapter 2

Sentient of Stone

"Arg. Get off me!" thundered a hidden voice.

Mariska quickly scurried to the ground as the rock shuddered and rolled onto its side.

Was the rock alive!?

Fear had her paralyzed. Her heart was racing. And she was staring.

Again a bellowing, slow voice rumbled: "What are you doing standing on an injured person like that? Do you not have any common sense?"

Mariska was sure the sound came from the moving rock, but she was still a little flabbergasted.

She could see its eyes now, bright and glowing red, looking directly into her grey eyes.

"Did you... the rock... just speak?" stammered Mariska.

"Well, I'm not a *rock*," barked the life form. "Rocks are impure, only good for building. I'm a Minerallian! I have a much more mineral-like chemical composition and organized atomic structure. Though I do have a few rock ancestors, we all do. And yes, I am the one who spoke," groaned the beast.

"Uh," was all that came out of Mariska's gaping mouth. She wasn't afraid of aliens, she'd seen plenty. The creature had just shocked her and she was at a loss for words. She fidgeted and kicked at a mushroom, clumsily missing it.

"You look frightened; is it me? Oh, it's me," quoth the Minerallian. "I don't mean to scare you, I'm just a little crusty and very grumpy; much to the chagrin of the elders."

The rock being slowly sat up, grinding, moving as though it ached.

It was huge.

And handsome. Having big shoulders with chunky, translucent, bright red rectangles on top, illuminated by the sunlight. In fact it had two sets of shoulders, and subsequently four arms! The lower appendages had dainty hands, the upper arms solid and thick mandibles. The rock giant was sharply coloured with veins of silvery-black and chunks of bright red running throughout its body.

The creatures's head was a big slab of carved stone with deep set eyes and a thick jaw that opened and closed when it spoke. But its head wasn't on the top of its body, it was mid-way down its chest, protruding forwards, as though the large set of shoulders were stacked on top of its neck.

The sentient rock started rotating its arms and shoulders as though stretching, and Mariska could see that its joints looked like masterfully sculpted stone gears. They swivelled and articulated as the rock giant moved its appendages.

How did I mistake this creature for a boulder? thought Mariska. Now that she could see all of it, and it hadn't immediately attacked her, her shock started to abate. She realized it was chanting quietly in a deep guttural tone.

"Are you hurt?" asked Mariska tentatively.

After a few seconds the chanting stopped. The Minerallian replied, "I expect I'll be QX; just going through my calming routine. It's supposed to help me be a little more stoic. Doesn't work very well."

"Your ship is in bad condition," said Mariska.

Its big, boulder head rotated towards the ship. "Yes, it does look particularly desolate. Are you the pilot of the ship that I almost collided with?" asked the Minerallian.

"Yep."

"I'm sorry about that; I'm not good at this whole

piloting starships thing. Is your vessel QX?"

Mariska sighed in disappointment and started to relax as much as she could with another being around. "It's not flight-worthy, but think I can repair it with a little work. At least it appears that we both survived. I'm Mariska Arisia." She thrust her hand towards the rock creature as a sign of friendship.

"Rhodochrosite Tetrahedrite Quartz Hallvarður, at your service," he responded, taking her comparatively small hand in one of his secondary palms and shaking it gently. "But you can call me Hal."

Though he was made of rock, or something rock-like, his grip wasn't destructively strong; there was a lot of control in his tiny, stone, gear-joints.

Now that Mariska's adrenalin was back to normal, she remembered how hot she was. Moving into the shadow of the bulking wreak, she grabbed her water bottle and took another few gulps.

The small talk was getting boring, so Mariska closed herself off and started reviewing her plan, trying to determine the next step. Her hopes of this ship being flyable were crushed. Maybe they could salvage some parts from the vessel and repair *Stellar Hermes*. But she would never ask for parts. She didn't take handouts.

Mariska wanted to get back on track for her delivery— getting her package to its destination was paramount.

Staring downwards into nothing, she spoke the next steps of her plan: "I think we should go back to my ship and repair it. Maybe we can find a nearby spaceport. And as long as we don't fly too crazily, I think we'll be QX." Mariska's eyes searched up the now standing and towering rock giant towards his face, waiting for a response. She added, "Although, I think you may be just a bit too big for *Stellar Hermes.*"

"Don't worry too much about fitting me into your ship. Let me try my subspace radio first; maybe I can get some help," said Hallvarður. He lumbered into his downed vessel, shaking the ground as he moved. Mariska could hear him huffing and grunting as he rummaged around inside.

Hallvarður reappeared in the hatchway and grumbled: "I can't get it to work. Let's get on with your plan." Hal absently looked around the interior of his ship and asked Mariska: "Maybe we should salvage this pile of trash for your ship? Anything you need?"

In the excitement of Hal asking her exactly what she wanted, words burst from Mariska's mouth: "Yeah, I could use a capacitive fluxeon ionizer! Though we'd have to carry it all the way back."

"Good. I've got one of those. And as for carrying things, you may have noticed I'm quite large," joked Hallvarður. He disappeared into the hatch and Mariska followed quickly behind.

The interior of Hal's ship was unremarkable, in fact it looked like a big, empty cargo freighter with tie-down mesh on every wall. To her left was the entrance for the cockpit and to her right a large, open door for accessing the cargo chamber. In front of her on the opposite wall was an array of tools: hydro-hammers, auto-wrenches, electro-laser drills, sonic screwdrivers, spanners, nuclear welders, grapple rays, glass formers, and more. Below the tools was a chest of drawers and immediately beside that was a dinged up tug-bot. It looked like it had been through a war; one of its pushers was broken beyond repair. The whole ship was very pedestrian, just how Mariska liked it, and she wondered if the ship reflected its pilot the same way *Stellar Hermes* reflected her.

The cargo area towards the rear was dirty and dark and dusty. A thick metallic powder sparkled gold, silver, copper, ruby, emerald, and turquoise in the little beams of light from the doorway. It looked like a beautiful treasure had recently been stolen from the room. Mariska gaped and blinked involuntarily.

"Yeah, shiny, eh," remarked Hallvarður, adding, "It's a mining freighter after all, we used to collect minerals and ores for creating new Minerallians—but it hasn't been used in years," Hal added with a sad tone. That comment piqued Mariska's interest. She made a mental note to ask him more about it later. Hallvarður continued, "There's the ionizer for you; it's junky and old, just like this whole bucket, but it works," pointing with one of his massive upper arms.

Mariska was a little disappointed with the ionizer—hopefully it didn't show on her face. It was older than the one on *Stellar Hermes* that she wanted replaced, but it was better than nothing.

"Thanks," she said in a quiet voice, adding: "I really appreciate it."

"No worries; this mining truck was ready for the scrapyard anyways," responded Hal in a deep voice. "Anything else interest you, or shall we be on our way?"

Mariska didn't respond—no extra words were needed. She stepped outside, took a deep breath, a fresh gulp from her water bottle, grabbed up her backpack, and started heading back up the steep slope with Hallvarður following, carrying the ionizer like a barrel under one of his big arms.

Mariska was a fast walker by most peoples' standards, but compared to Hallvarður she was a snail. His huge lumbering legs took long strides forward, thundering when they touched the ground. He seemed to take a step and wait for her, but without concern for her speed. She thought, maybe, he was enjoying the company.

The sun glinted off the different veins of colour in his body. NAN-C, floating behind, remarked how impressive he looked in the sun, but Hal just shook off the compliment.

The Bed of Basidiomycota was still as marvellous the second time. Hallvarður seemed to take particular pleasure in squashing the fungi with his heavy, stone feet—each time making a growling sound.

If she timed it just so, she could hide in Hal's shadow every few steps, but it didn't help with the heat too much. She stopped a moment to take the last gulp of water from her bottle and looked up at the triple suns shining down on the mushroom plain.

It was late in the afternoon, still extremely hot and sticky.

She noticed that the suns were all low in the sky and wondered if there would be a nighttime on this mysterious planet.

The suns were all a part of the two combined planetary systems she lived in. It was said that eons ago, the binary star system, aptly named The First System, collided with a smaller planetary system named The Old System. With all the weird gravitational pulls in her trinary system, from the orbiting suns and stresses of The Big Merge, some of the planets had very eccentric orbits.

Each sun was a different size and colour. The First System's binaries were Ataksak, an F-Class yellow-white star, and its companion, Akycha, a G-Class yellow star. The Old System, which orbited on the outskirts of the binary pair, was formed around Ignirtoq, a K-Class orange star.

This is the closest Mariska had ever been to Ignirtoq, and that excited her a little. The Old System was at the far outside of the primary stars, following a very eccentric orbit, and little was known about it.

. . .

Mariska was worrying about the silence between her and Hallvarður, concerned that he may find it awkward. Doing what was socially expected of her, she took a deep breath and said: "So, you mined to create new Minerallians?"

"Well… yes, children, you know; but we haven't in many years, ever since Minerallia started slowly losing altitude, descending towards this infested planet. It really irks me, if you haven't noticed."

She had noticed.

Hal continued: "The elders are disappointed with my meddling where I don't belong; they've just given up." Mariska could tell by his tone that it was a sensitive topic, so she didn't continue with the subject.

"It's quite the weather, *a tiny bit warm,*" remarked Mariska, trying to follow the common small talk subjects: job, weather, family, interests.

Uh, this is horrible, thought Mariska.

"Is the heat bothering you, Mariska? I hadn't noticed it."

"Yes, I'm soaked with sweat," she admitted—and she was. Her chest and stomach were wet, her hair a sopping mess. And her underwear…

As they continued walking, Mariska was getting a little anxious and weak. She was only half listening to NAN-C's chattering about the mushrooms, but even that was getting annoying. So she flipped the mute switch on NAN-C's handheld remote.

She retreated into silence for a while, hoping it wouldn't be awkward.

The distance back to her ship seemed so much further than the trip out.

Her legs were turning to jelly.

Everything was blurry; she wasn't sure if it was the haze or her own eyes.

Mariska kept plodding along, not hearing anything, not seeing anything, only feeling the heat.

She needed to get back to her ship.

She needed to deliver her cargo.

Her lips were cracked and dry, aching for water.

It had been hours of walking in the heat. Mariska was sure she should have made it back to her ship by now. Or at least have seen it through the haze. *Could Hal not see further up that high?*

In desperation, she flipped NAN-C back on, and its voice burst out: "Mariska the ship is gone! I would have told you earlier but you had me muted. We passed the crash site on our left about two-hundred metres ago."

Mariska immediately turned and sprinted with her last ounce of energy towards where her ship should have been. *How could my entire ship just disappear!?* She had to see it for herself.

When she reached the crash site, the *Stellar Hermes* was gone—all that remained was an empty crater.

Her eyes went completely blurry.

She noticed her balance failing.

She collapsed.

Everything went black—

Chapter 3

History of Hallvarður

Mariska awoke with a start, she looked around in every direction—*Stellar Hermes* was still gone.

What happened? she thought.

Immediately NAN-C cooed: "Mariska, love, I was really worried about you. You collapsed from exhaustion and dehydration." NAN-C's voice was a joy to hear.

Although Mariska was still a little groggy, she noticed Hallvarður sitting beside her. "Hey, Hal," she said.

"Hey, Mariska, glad to see you back," responded Hallvarður in his calm, deep voice. He added: "NAN-C, helped me out when you collapsed. She said you needed water so I used my *mystical earth powers*," he added with a wink, "to get a little drip of water going. I filled up your bottle and gave you some."

"Yes, he was quite a gentleman," remarked NAN-C. "You have only been unconscious for a couple hours, but I think you should get more sleep," murmured NAN-C. With an ever-loving tone NAN-C added: "Drink lots more water, dear. Hallvarður will fill your bottle if needed. Then eat some of the rations you packed." NAN-C was being motherly but Mariska didn't mind.

"I'm happy to sit and wait; I don't think we should travel when it's dark anyways," added Hal.

Mariska did what she was told: drank large gulps of water and ate some of the bland rations she stored in her backpack. She was feeling better than before fainting, but still very tired.

The sky wasn't completely pitch black. Along the horizon it was deep red, slowly fading through deep violet, and into black at the zenith. It looked like late dusk but Mariska felt sure it wasn't going to get any darker. It was cooler than before she passed out and the humidity had broken but it was still very warm.

She pulled the jacket out of her backpack and balled it up for a pillow.

"Thanks, guys," remarked Mariska as she laid down on her back. There were visible stars in about half of the heavens, and Mariska loved staring at the distant suns.

She knew she needed to sleep, but her mind wouldn't

relax. She was worrying about *Stellar Hermes*, and about her delivery, which was surely late. She was also thinking about Hal and hoping that she didn't bother him too much, hoping that he wasn't bored of her quiet company.

Mariska was worrying about what steps to take next, how to find her ship, where it had gone. All these ideas were flooding through her mind as she lay staring up at the twinkling stars.

The silence was inviting, but sleep wasn't coming easily.

She grabbed another draft of water and concentrated on relaxing her body. She started with her toes, feeling every joint, every muscle, making them comfortable. She worked up her shins, tensing her muscles, then releasing; onto her thighs, and hips, tensing and releasing. Getting to her lower back, she realized the cargo tagger holstered to the back of her utility belt was digging in; she wriggled around to take it off. Next up: her stomach and chest, which were usually relaxed. But she couldn't find a comfortable place for her hands. At least the fungi provided a soft surface. She finally made it to her face and eyes, stretching open her face muscles and squashing them tight, trying to relax.

This technique usually worked well to help calm her mind. To focus on her being, to focus on her breathing— but it required lots of concentration to hide the other worrying thoughts.

She finally felt the relaxed state she needed to fall asleep. She rolled onto her right side and drifted off.

Mariska woke up at dawn and sat up. Only one of the suns was fully visible, the second just peeking over the horizon. She felt refreshed.

Halvarður was standing nearby, next to the crash crater.

Heeding NAN-C's warning from the night before, Mariska drank a few more sips of water. She noticed that the bottle had been refilled and thought: *I need to ask Hal how he does that.* She grabbed a snack bar from her backpack and gobbled it down hungrily.

Getting to her feet, the muscles in her lean legs aching from the day before, she stretched her arms and shoulders, and slowly walked over to where Hal was standing. "Mornin' Hal."

He turned his large torso towards her and said, "Hey, Mariska, glad to see you're up and ready. I have something to show you." Hallvarður bent down to the edge of the crater and pointed at the ground with one of his small lower hands. "Right there, some residue, from Mycotazens, vile creatures."

"You think that's what took my ship?" questioned Mariska.

"Yes, definitely; they're scavengers," responded Hal in a gruff, almost disgusted voice. He added: "Now we just need to figure out where they went."

"QX. Have you been to this planet before?" asked Mariska with a hint of trepidation in her voice.

"Yep; Mycota is its name. I can only stand to be here for short periods of time, and I don't really know this area very well. My home world is one of the two moons of this planet, actually." Hallvarður clearly had a negative history with Mycota and its inhabitants, it was plain in the sound of his voice.

Mariska was too concerned with finding her ship to pursue the subject any further. She bounded to the southern side of the crater, eagerly looking for a clue. She didn't know what to look for: something out of place, something unusual, something new. She was looking for any evidence she could find.

"Do the Mycotazens leave that residue wherever they go?" she asked Hal.

"Yes, but only if they've stayed in one place for a while. So we can't use it to track their movements."

"Well, that idea is shot," sighed Mariska. *Maybe*, she thought, *there are some drag marks or depressions in the ground from the vehicles that had moved my ship.* Looking around she didn't see anything immediately near the crater, but a few metres away she noticed a small mound of dirt and some smushed fungi. She posited: "What about this, Hal? A drag mark?"

He lumbered towards her and looked down, "Yeah, looks like it. Lets see if we can figure out their direction."

Mariska walked away from the drag mark, at about the same angle from the crash gorge, for a dozen or so metres. She called back to Hallvarður: "There's another one over here!"

Hal took a couple of long, thundering strides and was immediately beside her, peering down. "Yep, looks like they went that way," pointing to the south-west.

Mariska was slightly relieved. She had a concrete plan.

She jogged back to the crater, buckled on her belt, grabbed her backpack, shoved her water bottle and jacket inside, and ran back to Hallvarður to follow the trail.

The heat was much more bearable than on the previous day. And the walk was pleasant. The ground cover was similar to the Bed of Basidiomycota but because the air was clearer she could see that ahead the plants were starting to get taller.

Hal was taking his usual long stride, then pausing for her to catch up. He seemed to be in a foul mood today.

NAN-C was dictating the different fungi that she

could recognize: "Elfin saddles, ghost fungi, common stinkhorns, stalked scarlet cups, chanterelles, scarlet elf caps, violet-grey boletes, a spotted tricholoma."

As they got further away from the crash site, they recognized fewer and fewer mushrooms. Mariska noticed an inky coloured stalk came up to her waist; a cluster of tiny, bright green mushrooms; a brown bulbous looking sack with smaller mushrooms inside—she just couldn't believe the varieties.

They were able to follow the trail easily: about every dozen metres or so there would be another indentation and another series of crushed fungi. Though it helped them track *Stellar Hermes*, Mariska was worried about her ship: hopefully this banging on the ground hadn't damage it any further.

As they proceeded, Hallvarður's fits of aggression towards the mushrooms started to become more and more violent. He was stomping on them, kicking them into the air, crushing them with his fist, swiping his arms around to chop them off. Something about the fungi really angered him.

Mariska was getting worried about the capacitive fluxeon ionizer Hal was carrying under his arm; concerned that he may drop it with all his flailing. And that would really ruin her plan for getting off this planet. They had been walking in silence, except for Hal's grunting and huffing. Mariska wanted to calm him down and remembered that some people liked to talk about their problems. *Here it goes*, she thought to herself.

"Hey, Hal, are you alright? You seem a little... off today," asked Mariska, hoping not to insult him.

He kicked another juicy looking mushroom and looked towards her. "Well, my people have a... kind of... hate relationship with the Mycotazens," replied Hallvarður. "They forced us to abandon our homes. The Minerallians used to live on Mycota too, but the viral 'Shroom people wouldn't leave us alone. They kept growing on our bodies, eventually killing us by breaking us apart with their roots.

"We decided the moon was our last chance. Since we don't need an atmosphere to survive—and the 'Shrooms do—we could live there peacefully. And we have been for years. But any day now we're going to lose our homes again; the moon is losing altitude, from a collision with a rogue asteroid. Its orbit is going to completely destabilize, crashing into this planet.

"My people have just given up on life. We stopped making children, stopped caring for our cities, stopped mining—stopped living. Everyone is ready to die. But I won't accept that!"

Mariska noticed that Hal's body language was a little better, hopefully the talking was helping because she really didn't want the ionizer damaged. She was a good listener. Talking wasn't her thing.

"I'm really sorry to hear that," she added in her best conciliatory tone. "I don't understand why they would just give up like that."

"Neither do I," replied Hal in a gruff voice, "they say the end is inevitable."

Hallvarður continued: "I believe we can continue on, that we can thrive somewhere else, if we can just get off the moon before we all plummet to our death. But many of the elders are against my cause. They say I'm meddling with powers I don't understand."

Dejected, Hal dropped, to the ground with a loud, vibrating boom. Mariska plopped down beside him and started to take a drink of water. It was empty. Hoping not to repeat the events of the day before, she asked for help, as hard as it was to do: "Hal... could you get me some more water?"

"Why yes," he replied.

He set down the ionizer and took her water bottle in one of his smaller hands. Hal stood up, turned around and shimmied his feet a little. He bent over and, with a big hand, palmed along the ground.

Slam—

He smashed his fist on the ground, cracking it. There was a deep rumble and stone spikes shot out of the ground sprouting a little fresh water spring.

He turned to her, with what she could guess was a grin, and said: "We Minerallians have a connection with the ground and stones; we can sense the composition."

That explains it, thought Mariska.

He handed the water bottle back to her after filling it up, and sat back down. She took it and said thank you.

"I'm sorry if I haven't been a very good companion," remarked Hallvarður, "sometimes my anger gets the best of me. I'll try to be a little more cordial, maybe talk some more, if you'd like."

Talk more!? No, thought Mariska. But, instead she responded: "I don't mind the silence; it's almost comforting."

"That's QX with me."

Mariska's anxiety of being around other people and the stress of social pressure to talk lessened. *I guess the silence is good with him too.*

So they both sat there quietly, basking in the light of the three suns.

Hal was murmuring his calming ritual.

Mariska looked forward, in the direction they were headed.

She could see in the distance, many kilometres away, that the flora was really tall, mimicking a forest.

NAN-C chirped: "Just left of your hand, hon, there's a delicious looking white truffle. They're edible; try it out."

Mariska looked over and saw a mushroom about eight centimetres wide. She plucked it and turned it around in her hand. Reluctantly, she took a bite. It had a pungent taste, but not unpleasant; a nice change from the boring, fake tasting rations she had packed.

Mariska slowly finished the truffle and let Hal chant for a few more minutes, then stood up. "Ready to go?" she asked Hallvarður.

"Yeah, sure."

The two continued their walk towards the south-east, towards Mariska's ship.

· · ·

The fungi were getting taller the further they walked—and more exotic. Mariska even noticed some creatures flitting about the sky above them. The insectoids were approximately the length of her forearm, with fluffy, thick, long abdomens; long legs, bent below; two pairs of wings that fluttered and paused in quick motions, glinting in the sunlight; and a series of pincers below their compound eyes. There were insects of different colours: pink, orange, magenta. The bugs hovered for a second then shot to another location, hovered, and moved. They seemed quite attracted to Hal and kept perching on his bright red shoulders. He'd swat at them but always missed.

Walking in silence was a treat for Mariska for very rarely did other beings just shut-up. It gave her plenty of time to think: about her cargo, nestled in her backpack; about her ship, stolen from her; about this mysterious planet, covered in mushrooms; about the amazing flying bugs hovering above their heads.

After several hours of walking, and a few snack breaks, the mushroom forest was looming ahead of them, getting closer by the minute. The walk was more difficult, with taller fungi and grasses with tough stalks hampering their path. In some places the plants were taller than Mariska.

In her typical clumsy fashion she kept tripping on small roots, losing her balance, and almost falling.

After a while, they reached a lull in the taller ground coverings. Immediately in front of the two companions, thirty metres away, was a massive wall of ginormous, imposing mushroom trees.

The interior of the fungi forest looked dim—and ominous.

They both stood there and gawked at it.

Hallvarður broke the silence: "I've got a bad feeling about this."

Chapter 4

Forest of Fungi

It was late afternoon, the suns were high in the sky but it was still dim inside the forest. There were some patches of light streaming through the canopy, highlighting motes floating in the air. Overall, the limited amount of light was to be expected from a dense jungle.

It was cooler inside, with gusts of chilly wind that flowed between the prototaxites. Out of the corners of her eyes Mariska saw quick streaking shadows and movements. The forest had a disconcerting silence about it, broken intermittently with rustling plants or distant, kooky warbling sounds of what she imagined could only be alien birds.

All around the twosome were tall, striking mushrooms

and fungi trees, the tops of which were metres above their heads. Huge mushrooms with bulbous bases with large curling vines wrapped around the thick stems; spore sacks hanging down from mushroom caps, daring them to touch; rings fluttering like capes of super villains.

The whole forest seemed to react to their passage: leaning into them, bending away from them; some fungi would snap shut, startling Mariska; some fungi would open wide, inviting in a snack; huge puff balls would explode in clouds of earthy smoke as they stepped near; vines would inch forward towards their feet or constrict more tightly against their symbiotic fungi.

The strange movements sent chills up Mariska's spine.

She was sure there were weird creatures following them. Glowing sinister eyes would peer around trunks and stems, sounds of tiny skittering legs would echo in the darkness, and the clacking of nefarious mandibles would rattle through the plants. But she could never get a clear view.

The deeper they went into the forest, the more odd things got: mushrooms would pull up out of the ground and run away on their mycelium; stink horns would puff out the most horrendous smells; mushrooms with nets would contract around mysterious insects—everything seemed alive!

The eerie fungal forest made Mariska uneasy—but, for

the two adventurers, it was a necessary hurdle in their quest.

. . .

Mariska and Hallvarður walked slowly, tunnelling their way through the thick grove. It was silent between them, as they concentrated on the arduous task. Randomly, one of them would break the silence with a quick staccato: "Did you see that?" or "I don't like the sound of that," or "I swear that vine just tried to grab my leg!"

Mariska was enjoying the silence—and the exertion. It was taking her mind off her missing starship, her late cargo delivery—and the weirdness of this jungle.

With the silence calming his temper, Hal seemed to be thoroughly enjoying himself: tearing, ripping, shredding, and squashing every mushroom he could see.

Just as she thought they'd never see the end of the dense undergrowth, Hal and Mariska stumbled into a small clearing big enough for both of them to sit down. There was a clear patch of the late afternoon sunlight streaming to the forest floor.

Directly in the centre of the circular clearing was an odd looking fungi, just shorter than Mariska. On top, was a bundle of spherical, yellow and orange, mesh covered bulbs, each about the size of Mariska's head.

From a couple of the lower bulbs, sprouted a wrinkly, quivering membrane that oozed a gelatinous slime onto the surrounding ground. The stalk of the mushroom was withered and bent with wart-like protrusions.

Mariska looked at Hallvarður with an up-turned lip and said: "*That's appealing.*" He responded with a disgusted grunt. Getting the impression that the forest separated from this fungus for a reason, they sat as far from it as they could while still remaining in the sunlight.

Tiny, six-legged rodents scurried around the bottom of the mushroom, licking at the fallen slime. Some of the more adventurous ones climbed up the stalk and tried to feed directly on the hanging membranes; their attempts always failed as the membranes sucked inside with a gruesome slurp.

One of the critters came close to inspect Mariska. It was cuter than Mariska had expected, with a leathery, striped tail, and four deep black eyes. It sat there staring at her, enthusiastically rubbing the slime around its mouth. Mariska moved, startled it, and it darted away.

Though the forest surrounded them, this little clearing was a nice relief from the imposing gloom they'd been suffering through. Mariska drank and ate while they sat there resting. She offered him a snack but he declined, saying that he didn't need to eat.

"Thanks for coming along," remarked Mariska, after

she finished a gulp of water.

"No worries. I want to get off this life-sucking ball of fungus as much as you do."

And that was the extent of their conversation in the clearing, both of them appreciating the others' silent company.

After a suitable break, they continued on the treacherous trek to find the abducted *Stellar Hermes*.

Since they had entered the forest, there was no sign of the trail. NAN-C was keeping them on course by following the same line. It was their best option: they had thought about going around the forest, but couldn't see any end, and were worried they wouldn't be able to pick up the trail on the other side. And Mariska, of course, worried about how long it would take, and how it would further delay her delivery.

Now that they were deep inside the forest, though, both of them thought it may have been better to go around—the forest was the nemesis of speed.

They had just entered a particularly gnarly patch of forest

and Mariska's klutziness was literally tripping her up. She just couldn't stay on her feet: roots would pop out of the ground, vines would snake around her ankles, trunks would lurch to the side when she tried to brace herself.

She was getting further behind Hallvarður with every step. It was as though the forest was against her.

A vine grasped tightly around her shins, knocking her on her stomach. Her backpack burst open, the cargo box tumbled out, and its lid popped open, revealing the contents.

Hal heard her fall and turned to help, but was awestruck by the contents of her cargo box.

As he bent down to grab it a gigantic fungal net dropped from the canopy and scooped him up. He fought, punched, kicked, but to no avail.

Mariska jumped up and raced towards the captured Hal, calling out to him, but the fungus net scuttled away on its tiny roots.

Mariska ran as fast as she could to reach Hallvarður, but she couldn't keep up. The forest was holding her back, aiding the fungus's retreat.

The fungus trap was getting away.

She dropped to her knee, reached behind her back and grabbed the cargo tagger she used to track all her packages with.

Balancing the small device in one hand and using her

second hand to tripod against her knee, she took careful aim. Moving targets were not her thing.

She shot!

The tracking disc missed and bounced off a hanging vine.

Hallvarður was getting out of reach, calling for her help.

She had one chance left. She fired again—

The disc hit Hal directly in the abdomen.

Relief flowed through her as Hal disappeared into the distance, the vines and fungi closing off behind the net-fungus's retreat.

Mariska was alone.

Chapter 5

Jumble of Junk

Mariska was finally on her own—too bad the situation wasn't a little better. She enjoyed being alone, it renewed her energy, helped clear her head, and relaxed her. That's why she wanted to be a courier: lots of time by herself while flitting about the planetary system. But her family didn't understand. She wasn't really an outcast—they loved her dearly—but they thought her quietness was an issue. Mariposa, her sister, was the outgoing, loveable one in the family—exactly what her parents wanted.

Mariska's parents weren't too happy when she told them she wanted to be a courier. They had planned for her to become a scientist, like Mariposa—but that didn't fit with her introversion. The idea of having to talk to people all day, to give presentations, and meet new people every day. It grated against her soul.

And it wasn't that Mariska didn't like people—she did—but only in small doses. Being around other people was exhausting. Hal was different though.

Still, Mariska loved science and learning, but she loved doing those things on her own. That's why being a courier was perfect for her: she would meet people every few days, for short periods of time, then get back to her ship, recharge, and learn—alone.

Even though Mariska was by herself right now, and feeling a little relieved that the social pressure was completely removed, she was still upset about Hal getting shroom-napped.

After Hal had disappeared, she stood in place for a couple minutes in a daze: What was she to do next? Her plans kept getting disrupted and ruined. NAN-C pointed out that *Stellar Hermes* and Hallvarður were both in the same direction, so Mariska placed the cargo back in its box, tucked it in her backpack, and started following the trail.

Mariska was walking forward, deep in her thoughts about her life, about Hal, about her ship, and about her cargo—which Hal seemed very interested in. *I wonder why he was mesmerized by the cargo? It just looks like an ancient ornament.*

The sky was getting darker above. *It must be late in the evening now and the suns must be near to setting.* But inside the forest the light remained similar to the day; fungi everywhere started glowing with bioluminescence—it was an amazing site. Mushrooms on the ground would create little light paths, lichens on the stems glowed green and blue, brackets would glow red or purple. Every direction Mariska looked glowing fungi lit up the forest.

In fact, in the dark, the forest was more friendly: it had stopped preventing her passage and became much easier to move through. There were less creepy staring eyes, less evil moving vines, a generally less ominous feeling. It was just a pleasant glowing forest of fungi.

NAN-C, floating above her left shoulder, was also mesmerized by the bioluminescent fungi, the orb had to start telling Mariska about them: "bitter oysters, gerronema viridilucens, tsukiyotake, slippery mycena, jack-o'-lantern mushrooms, lilac bonnets..."

Mariska was getting tired of walking—and just tired in general—she'd spent half her day in the forest and the other half on the mushroom plains. She really just wanted to get back to *Stellar Hermes*, have a long, hot shower, and stay there alone for the next few days. She was a creature of habit.

But, she didn't have a choice, so she kept trudging along in the forest, admiring the glowing fungi trees and thinking. At this moment her thoughts jumped again to Hal and to his face when he saw the cargo. *What was it? Had he seen something like that before?* Those questions couldn't be answered without him.

"NAN-C, any idea how much longer until we get out of this forest? I'd rather not be in here all night," asked Mariska impatiently.

"Actually, the flora seems to be thinning and getting shorter. I would guess that it is not too far ahead."

After NAN-C responded, Mariska noticed that she could see the edge of the forest. She quickened her pace. Maybe there would be something different when she reached the edge.

Racing through the fungi she finally reached the tree line. A couple of kilometres away, across a mushroom field, she could see something faint in the evening dusk, surrounded by tall bioluminescent mushrooms.

Mariska pulled out her macrobinoculars and looked through them. She saw piles of stuff; though fairly organized into rows. Zooming closer and turning up the low-light knob, Mariska could see that it was a junkyard full of mechanical parts, spaceship components, engines, stabilizers, seats, everything.

She scanned the whole yard from right to left, regarding all the different piles separated by paths. Just as she was nearing the far left something caught her eye, a shape she would recognize anywhere: *Stellar Hermes*.

Mariska's stomach dropped, she could see her home! And it was still in one piece. She felt a renewed sense of relief and a burst of energy washed over her. Mariska started towards it, as fast as her lanky legs could take her.

Her heart was racing with excitement and she wasn't paying attention to much else.

"Dear, we should be careful. I am picking up movement around the ship and the junkyard. It could be under guard." But Mariska didn't want to hear it, she had a mission now: Get to *Stellar Hermes* as fast as possible. Hopefully it was in no worse condition than the last time she'd seen it.

She was getting close to *Stellar Hermes*, the glowing mushrooms bathed the ground with a decent amount of light. All around her were towering piles of dreck, scavenged by the Mycotazens.

"Mariska! Wait!" called NAN-C. "There are creatures moving around." But Mariska was focussed, pushing forward.

A mushroom-beast pounced on her from the side, knocking her completely to the ground. It was large, slime dripping from its gills, it had three legs, and was growling. It stood on her chest pinning her down, looking into her eyes through evil, beady, black slits.

Mariska snapped out of her trance and hit the mushroom in the side. It didn't work. Spores just burst into the air and rained down onto her; the guard creature's slime dripped onto her face.

She screamed and wriggled, trying to free herself from its strong legs.

Mariska was kicking her feet and flailing her arms. Her hand grazed against the mushroom's gills—they were soft and spongy.

She grabbed hold with both hands and pulled with all her might, easily tearing away handfuls of frail gills.

The mushroom let out a yelp and jumped off her chest, shaking its head. It was enough for her to get back to her feet.

She was too close to *Stellar Hermes*. This beast wasn't going to stop her.

She bolted to her left, trying to get away from the guard. It ran after her and clamped its mouth onto her pant leg, tripping her. She slammed to the ground on her chest.

Mariska kicked with her free leg, connecting with the mushroom's head. It released her leg.

She got up and ran towards a junk pile with the creature close behind. Clambering and tripping up the loose pile of garbage, pieces fell away as she ascended. The beast came close on her heels, but couldn't climb.

Mariska's leg slipped and a large brick-like object plummeted off the pile and hit the beast—not slowing it down.

It was clawing chunks of the pile away at the base, trying to get her. Heavy pieces were coming off, and the pile started to destabilize.

Slowly at first, then picking up speed, the pile of junk collapsed and fell. Mariska lost her footing and tumbled forward just as the pile toppled over, crushing the mushroom.

Mariska lay on top of the downed pile, bruised and battered, but still alive. *Well, that was easy*, thought Mariska.

Now, she was ready to heed NAN-C's warnings.

She gingerly stood up, aching, and walked towards *Stellar Hermes*. All her senses heightened by adrenaline, she said: "NAN-C, a little more warning next time would be nice."

"Yes, of course, my darling," the computer responded with a hint of sarcasm.

. . .

Mariska walked around the outside of her ship, inspecting

it. She admired the deep yellow stripes, she had painted them herself; the protruding cockpit, with its big transparisteel windows; the sloped forward mandibles; the side dark matter collectors; and the two large rear thrusters, with their misaligned ailerons. *Stellar Hermes* looked good and had no more damage than when she last saw it. The banging on the ground from being transported here hadn't left any new marks.

Her ship sent tingles down her spine.

The starship was still resting on the ground without the landing gear extended, just as she left it. She palmed a bio-feedback knob on the side, unlocking the landing ramp and opening it silently. Mariska walked up the ramp, with NAN-C floating behind. Getting to the top, she closed and locked the door—cutting off the outside world.

Mariska looked around the inside of her small ship from left to right, it wasn't much bigger than a bachelor apartment—perfect for just her. To her left was her high bed with shelving below; next to that was the small bathroom with a sink, toilet, and shower; the door to the cockpit came next with storage units on either side; across the room was a small table with two chairs, scattered with books that had fallen out of the overhead bookshelf; and right beside that, across from the "bedroom," was a tiny kitchenette, with a small refrigerator, a sink, and a tiny cooking unit. And finally to her right was a hatchway that led back to the engine room.

Things were jostled about from the crash a couple days ago, but everything was perfect. She felt safe here inside—and she was completely alone.

She immediately stripped and jumped in the shower to clean off the grime of the past few days—and the slime of the past few minutes. Long, hot showers were always serene for her, giving her a quiet time to really interact with her thoughts; sometimes she worried about being in the shower for too long, but rarely did that stop her from standing longer.

She thought about Hal and about what her next steps should be: should she save him or just fix up her starship and deliver her cargo? Fixing up *Stellar Hermes* was very inviting; this junkyard had to have everything she needed and it seemed very well organized.

Hal is a big guy, he can look after himself.

But saving him is the right thing to do.

I really need the money to fix up Stellar Hermes.

Would I even get paid for this job now that I'm so late?

What is the cargo, anyways? Why was Hal so interested in it?

Should I fix Hermes *and save my reputation or should I rescue Hal?*

All of these thoughts flowed through her mind as the

hot water cascaded over her body, each thought pausing for a moment while Mariska pondered.

After standing in the shower for a long time, thinking, she dried herself off, got into bed, sealed the blankets tight around her, took a quick look out the porthole above her head, then promptly fell asleep.

Chapter 6

Installation of Ionizers

Mariska awoke the next morning at the break of dawn, refreshed and ready to take on the day. She had finally decided what she was going to do—everything. She would take a few hours to fix her ship this morning, assuming she could find an ionizer, since the other one had disappeared with Hal; go rescue Hal this afternoon; drop him off at home this evening, if she could fit him into her ship; and be at the Terrack-Pycon Ship Yards by morning tomorrow to deliver her cargo.

Mariska got dressed and set out to program NAN-C on a seeking course to search the junkyard for a capacitive fluxeon ionizer and subspace communication array parts, and report back if she found more of those beasts. She opened the top hatch and released NAN-C on the quest before sitting down, alone, in her kitchenette, to eat a breakfast of fresh fruit and nuts.

While NAN-C was gone for a couple hours systematically scouring the junkyard, Mariska had plenty of time to realign the thrust vectoring ailerons on the tail of her vessel; they would have to be in good working order if she planned to actually manoeuvre her vessel off this planet.

She was enjoying working on *Stellar Hermes*, while being careful not to attract unwanted attention. She was happy that she had a concrete plan, but a little nervous about rescuing Hallvarður this afternoon.

She would have felt really badly leaving Hal here to fend for himself, so she was happy with the plan she had concocted. Having a good reputation was great, but abandoning your acquaintances for it was probably a bad choice.

NAN-C returned with some good news and some bad news: There was a pile of ionizers a few rows over and many columns up, but there were quite a few mushroom-guard-beasts stalking about the pathways. There weren't any useful parts for the radio which stressed Mariska. She felt she needed to call her client to explain her lateness.

Mariska knew she had to go get the ionizer. She had to rescue Hal and deliver her cargo, and to do that she really needed the ionizer. She reached into the cabinet under her bed and grabbed a tranq-gun. Real guns were not her thing.

Using NAN-C, Mariska checked that there were no beasts in the proximity of her ship. She lowered the landing ramp and pushed out the repulsor-sled to help carry back the ionizer.

Cautiously, pushing the sled, Mariska moved along the pathways towards the stack of ionizers. NAN-C scouted out in front for guards while Mariska watched NAN-C's cameras intently on the hand terminal, hoping not to repeat the attack from the day before.

The meandering paths looked well worn, with very few machine tracks; they looked like organic trails. Mariska noticed there were no mushrooms in the junkyard. No mushrooms!

As she had surmised the day before, the junkyard was immaculately organized. Each pile held components of a single function, and of many different models. She passed a heap of wheeled landing gear, a pile of sledded landing gear, a stack of water landing gear, a mound of hovering landing gear, a stockpile of space-grappling gear, and a hoard of asteroid latching gear—every component possible had a place.

And the junkyard was huge, every direction she looked there were pyramids of components, piles of gizmos, and heaps of doohickeys.

Mariska managed to make it to the stack of ionizers without seeing any guards. She started rummaging through, trying to keep quiet and not attract any unwanted guests. Mariska was hoping to find a newer model capacitive fluxeon ionizer in good condition, but everything was looking pretty old and beat-up like the model Hallvarður had on his ship. Mariska kept digging.

While searching through the pile, NAN-C cooed: "Mariska, honey, there are two beasts getting close. Maybe you should quiet down for a minute and let them pass." Mariska stopped what she was doing and climbed up the pile to hide from the creatures.

Thankfully, they just walked by, seemingly unaware of her. Maybe they couldn't smell like the guard dogs on her home world.

After a couple minutes of silence, NAN-C gave her the QX and she continued hunting through the pile. Mariska couldn't find any newer models so she grabbed the best looking ionizer she could see and loaded it onto the repulsor-sled.

Mariska didn't like the idea of stealing the ionizer. But she rationalized her decision as a good cause.

Mariska started the walk back to *Stellar Hermes*,

pushing her load on the sled. The repulsor-lift hovered over the ground and took all of the weight, so she was really just guiding it along. There wasn't any physical exertion needed. And that was a good thing. This day, like every other day she had been on this planet, was hot and muggy. If she had to do more than just walk in the heat it would have been a struggle.

NAN-C chirped: "There is a creature up ahead and it is coming this way." Mariska, leaving the repulsor-sled behind, ducked behind a pile of junk and waited for the creature to pass. Hopefully it hadn't seen her.

The inquisitive beast, bigger than the one that attacked her the day before, moved slowly towards the sled.

It started circling around the repulsor-lift. Mariska sensed it knew something was wrong. The beast snapped its head up—

Mariska was slammed into the pile from behind; she could smell the same slime odour from the day before. *Did they trap me?*

Mariska turned around and there were two mushroom-beasts looking up at her.

Mariska stared at the two beasts and they stared back, ready to devour her.

Slowly she reached in her pants' pocket and slid her hand onto the grip of the tranq-pistol—

The creature on the left lunged for her chest.

She drew the tranq-gun and fired, hitting the beast directly in the body. It dropped like a sack.

The second beast was really close now. Mariska fired and missed. The beast lunged, almost knocking her to the ground, but she kept her footing and turned to back away.

The beast bent low, rage flowing through its body.

With shaky hands, she shot again, and missed again.

The mushroom-creature jumped forward, just short of Mariska, teasing her. *It's playing with its food*, thought Mariska.

With all three of its powerful legs, the beast charged forward, knocking Mariska to her back. The tranq-gun popped out of her hand and skittered just out of reach.

The creature was standing on her chest, oozing slime down onto her face. "NAN-C!" Mariska shouted, "Distract it!" NAN-C was more than just a computer and a sensor pad. The orb swooped down in front the monster's face and sent a micro laser blast towards the beast's eye.

With the distraction, the beast let just enough weight off Mariska. She reached for the tranq-pistol and fired it at the creature. It dropped, unconscious, knocking the breath out of her.

Wow, I'm getting a little tired of these things, thought Mariska.

Mariska pushed the huge beast off her chest and took a moment to catch her breath. She slowly got up and made her way over to the repulsor-sled to start the final trek back to her ship.

. . .

Mariska managed, uneventfully, to get the capacitive fluxeon ionizer installed on her ship and was ready to go find Hal. She made sure to pack some gear in her backpack—just in case.

She was worrying about the big guy. *Hopefully he was fine.* NAN-C had mentioned that he wasn't too far way, but that he was below their current plane. *Maybe he was underground?*

Walking through the junkyard was nerve-racking, especially after being attacked twice in as many days. NAN-C was probing ahead and behind. Mariska was being very careful: hugging the piles closely, walking slowly, making as little noise as she could. Thankfully, it was uneventful for the rest of the trip.

She reached the edge of the junkyard at the tip of a deep canyon. It stretched perpendicular to her in both directions, she couldn't see the ends. It was a few kilometres wide with steep rock faces.

Looking to the sides, Mariska could see that the canyon branched into different tributaries, some with dead ends, some looping back onto the original, primary canyon, and some creating a whole new chasm by themselves.

NAN-C chimed in: "Mariska, love, Hal is down in the canyon. From my sensors, he appears to be about four-hundred metres down and a kilometre to our right."

Carefully, Mariska crept up to the edge and peered over. Below her, hanging from the side of the canyon, was a mushroom city!

Chapter 7

City of Conks

Mariska stood at the edge of the cliff, looking over at the city, enjoying the breeze. She was impressed by the cityscape. Too bad she couldn't explore, she would have to get through it stealthily to save Hallvarður.

The city was hanging from the side of the canyon on awe-inspiring bracket mushrooms that created platforms for fungal buildings. She counted seven different terraces to the city, each at different heights, and each with blocks of fungal buildings on them.

The tallest buildings were only a few storeys high and the smaller ones were huts. The central bracket platform had the tallest buildings, and further from the centre, the buildings got smaller.

It was bustling: there were fungal life forms scurrying around the buildings, weird tripodal mushroom vehicles lumbering through the streets, and flying fungi soaring through the air above the buildings.

Hal is down there, thought Mariska, *but how am I going to get through all those beings without getting caught?*

There was an empty ramp leading down to the second mushroom platform from the left. She didn't have any gear to scale the cliff so it was her best chance to get down to the city.

Mariska launched herself forward and sprinted down the ramp, hoping she wouldn't be seen. She reached the bottom and ducked behind a small mushroom hut, confident she had gone unnoticed.

The hut, being made out of fungi, was squishy when she pressed against it. It looked like it was carved out of a clump of huge, spherical mushrooms yet standing back it may have looked like a really big, unappealing berry. There were other styles of huts: ones carved out of big puffball-like fungi, ones that looked like large swollen mushrooms, and pods that hung down from stems.

All the huts were small, likely one room on the inside. The doors weren't very high, about the height of Mariska's shoulders.

Mariska looked around, trying to figure out where to go next. According to NAN-C, to find Hal she needed to navigate three bracket platforms over. The platform she wanted was on the other side of the large, central core on a different level. *How do the mushroom people travel between the platforms?*

Mariska scurried between huts, making sure to stay close to the cliff wall, in the shadows. The platform she was on wasn't too wide, so it only took her a few minutes to get closer to its far edge.

Caves! As she was approaching the edge of the mushroom platform, she noticed a cave entrance in the side of the canyon. Looking further along the ravine wall, and above her, she saw another opening on the edge of the next terrace.

How am I going to get through the cave without being seen? thought Mariska. There were a couple of mushroom beings moving towards the entrance, and she worried there would be more inside.

The beings were cylindrical, like the stalks of mushrooms, shorter than Mariska, just lower than her chest. On the top of their stalks were transparent, bulbous spore sacks, with green, slit-eyes below. The creatures didn't have legs, it looked like they moved on their mycelium, like the net that had captured Hal. But they did have arms, each creature had a few that sprouted in every direction around their bodies.

Mariska decided to send NAN-C ahead through the

tunnel, to scope it out and alert her as to its safety. She gave the Mycotazens a couple minutes head start, then sent NAN-C gliding through the tunnel.

Mariska waited...

NAN-C popped out of the other side of the cave just after the two mushroom creatures scuttled slowly through the exit. NAN-C signalled back through the handheld: "After these two get further away, it is completely clear."

What luck! thought Mariska. She bolted through the curved tunnel as it ascended upwards to the neighbouring platform. After exiting the other side, Mariska dove behind a slightly bigger building. A little out of breath after the run, she thought, *Only two more platforms to go.*

Mariska prowled along the back of the new platform, pausing at each building to make sure she could cross to the next without being seen. She was edging towards another opening when a Mycotazen rounded the corner—

Mariska froze. The mushroom creature moved towards her. Mariska didn't want to get too close, so she slowly backed away, but the Mycotazen kept coming forward.

Her heart was racing, she didn't know what to do. The mushroom being was directly in front of her, looking forward—

But it just sauntered right by.

Mariska was stunned and confused, the Mycotazen had just completely ignored her. She stood in place for a moment, and watched the being disappear around another building.

Mariska was puzzled, the guard mushrooms earlier in the day were vicious towards her. These were not.

Hallvarður was waiting for her, so she cautiously walked forwards, passing a few more buildings without seeing any more Mycotazens.

Mariska peeked around another building—

A Mycotazen was standing there, facing her. This one noticed her. It tilted its head upwards and looked into her face. Mariska noticed its slits focus on her grey eyes. She quickly pulled her head around the corner of the building and stood for a minute hoping the creature would go away.

Mariska took another fast look. The mushroom being was still standing there but was no longer looking at her. Now was her chance. She bolted for the next building, looking back to make sure the mushroom life form didn't follow her—

She ran directly into another Myctoazen, knocking it to the ground. The mushroom creature got back up and walked right past her, as if completely oblivious to her.

Why are they ignoring me? thought Mariska. She was getting really suspicious. *Is it some sort of plan? Or a trap?*

While walking cautiously towards the next platform, she passed a few more Mycotazens. Each time they completely ignored her, seemingly disinterested in her or maybe letting her easily get to Hal to entrap her too.

She reached the edge of the platform she was on, and saw the central bracket terrace ahead. It was below the platform she was on, but many of the buildings were still taller.

To her right she spotted the connecting tunnel. There were Mycotazens everywhere: walking through it, leaning on the side of it, and standing around in groups.

Mariska was still concerned with the Mycotazens, so she sent NAN-C ahead to scan the tunnel. NAN-C reported that there were many more creatures inside the tunnel. *Should I wait here for the tunnel to clear?* thought Mariska. *Or should I risk just walking out, in the open, through the tunnel? They may just ignore me, if that's their plan.*

Mariska realized that it didn't matter why they weren't attacking her, she still needed to find Hallvarður.

So, it didn't look like she had much of a choice. Mariska strolled towards the cave, walking casually yet quickly, and made her way through the sloped tunnel and exited on the other side.

Realizing that they were going to ignore her, Mariska got a little braver. She needed to get to Hal, and if they were going to spring a trap, she might as well hurry up and get it over with.

She crossed to the large central bracket mushroom that had the most beings and traffic of all the terraces. Many of the buildings were taller: apartments, shops, eateries, and many other structures Mariska couldn't identify.

They were all different organic shapes, looking like they were created by some type of mushroom or fungus. There were short domed buildings, with round doorways; medium sized, bulb-shaped buildings on stalks, with steps up to them; and taller bunches of shoots, sticking into the sky. Next to the cliff was cluster of many smaller hut structures climbing down the side of the wall, joined by small pathways.

Right in the centre of the city was a more complex structure. It sat off the ground on six angular supports that rose upwards, being capped at the top with a spherical complex. Mycotazens were lounging around in groups underneath the structure around a trellised central pillar.

Mariska was wonderstruck at the mushroom city. The varieties and complexity of all the different fungi completely outmatched the Forest of Fungi and even the Bed of Basidomycota.

Mariska was walking quickly through the mushroom kingdom because she had a mission and a timeline. While all around her mushroom creatures, mushroom vehicles, and mushroom flyers went about their business.

When Mariska finally made it to the bracket mushroom platform that Hal was on, she started to walk more cautiously. *Surely the Mycotazens will care if I get too close to their prisoner.* She hoped she'd catch them off guard if they had planned a trap.

Mariska hung closely along the cliff while making her way towards where NAN-C said Hal would be. She rounded the side of a building and directly in the centre of a clearing, nestled next to the ravine wall, was Hallvarður, still trapped inside the net fungus.

Mariska quickly looked around and darted in behind Hal. *I'm getting good at this sneaking thing,* she thought, *I don't even think Hal saw me.* He was looking in the other direction, so Mariska whispered: "Psst, Hal."

He turned around, looked at her with his bright red eyes, and responded in his gruff voice: "Hey, Mariska. You found me. I knew you would." Mariska was happy to hear Hal's voice, even if it was a little grumpy.

Hal continued: "Took you long enough, though. I can't seem to break out of this net, the mesh is too strong. Frakin' 'Shrooms!"

Mariska could tell that Hal was in a foul mood. She would have been too if she were trapped in a cage. She said: "They just completely ignore me. I walked all the way through the city without them even looking."

"Well, yeah, they would. You're just another spongy life form, you don't have any *nutritious minerals* to grow on. They haven't got to me yet. I think this stinky fungus protects me; they can't seem to smell me through the odour."

"How are we going to get *you* out of here, Hal?"

"If you have a way to get me out of this rancid smelling net, I'm pretty adept at rock climbing," responded Hal, pointing upwards.

"QX. That'll work. I found *Stellar Hermes* and fixed it up before I came to get you. So if we can get back to it in one piece, I can get us off this planet."

Mariska reached into her utility belt and grabbed her box cutting laser. She seized a piece of the net and started slicing through it with the cutter. It was tough going, but Mariska was able to slash about a metre before Hal spoke: "Uh, hurry up, I think they've noticed!"

Mariska glanced up to see a bunch of the Mycotazens staring at her and Hallvarður. She hurried her pace, trying to slice through the net faster but the laser cutter was made for tape and cardboard. Mariska managed to cut a slice in the net about her height, still not big enough for Hal, when all around them, a crowd of 'Shrooms had formed, looking malevolent.

"They must be able to smell me now, through the break in the net," said Hallvarður.

Mariska finished cutting a hole as high as she could reach, then started cutting sideways to make it wider for Hal.

The Mycotazens were at her feet now, pushing against her, trying to get into the net. Hallvarður reached through with his large mandibles and started swatting them away, but it only encouraged their ravenous behaviour.

The Mycotazens started launching themselves at his arms, latching into the rock with their mycelium.

Hal couldn't wait any longer. He grabbed the sliced net with his large mandibles and stretched it apart as far as he could. Crouching and grunting, he squeezed through the too small hole.

Mycotazens were coming from everywhere, pushing, fighting, to get towards Hal. They were jumping in the air, latching onto his shoulders; running towards his large legs, and grabbing on. The Mycotazens were desperate to grow on his body.

Hal lunged a few steps forward, knocking a huge swath of the 'Shrooms flying. He turned around and grabbed Mariska tightly in his two smaller arms. He sprang towards the cliff face and grabbed a hold of the rocks with his large upper arms.

Myctoazens were climbing over each other, jumping

upwards trying to reach Hal. A bunch of them latched onto his feet. He was covered with fungi. Hal's lower legs were heavy with the creatures, and his red shoulders were covered in fungus.

Mariska was unhappy in his arms; she hated being helped. And she was hidden from the mass of mushrooms as Hal quickly ascended the rock face—she couldn't see anything.

Using his geological powers, he forced the cliff to adapt to his climb: rocks popped out for him to grab, holes sunk into the face for him to place his feet.

Mariska could partially see downwards, now that they were higher up. Hundreds of 'Shrooms were cluttered below, throwing themselves up into their air, trying to reach Hallvarður, but the duo were ascended up too high.

Hal climbed the cliff wall, grunting and moaning as they went. Mariska realized that all the fungal growths were hurting him, ripping apart his body.

Mariska could tell that the pain of these mushroom growths was bothering Hallvarður and it was slowing their progress. She could feel Hal urging his body upwards. His hands and feet were slipping on the rocks and the cliff was helping less.

The last fifty metres of the cliff were treacherous. Mariska worried that they were going to plummet to their death. Thankfully Hal fought through the pain and kept them both safe.

They finally crested the top, ready for the sprint through the junkyard to *Stellar Hermes*, but a small army of Mycotazens was waiting for them, pointing poisonous spore launchers directly at their faces.

Chapter 8

Endeavour of Escape

The beady eyes of the waiting Mycotazens stared menacingly at the companions. Just as the mushroom soldiers shot their poisonous spore weapons, Hallvarður spun around and crouched to protect Mariska.

There was a grumbling and cracking sound behind them. Mariska tried to peer beside Hal's bulking body, but he quickly jerked around. All the 'Shrooms were unconscious or gone, knocked away by the ground that Hallvarður had thrust upward with his earth powers.

Hal put Mariska down, and she took off running, yelling back: "Through the junkyard; on the far right side!" Hal thundered after her on his large rock legs, but not as quickly as the day before.

The fungal growths all over his upper shoulders and lower legs were slowing him down. He was grunting and moaning in pain. Pieces of mineral and rock were crumbling off his body. Hal called to Mariska: "Wait a second! I have to get rid of these frakin' 'Shrooms."

Mariska looked back at Hallvarður who was stooped over. He slowly straightened and his lower hands grasped hold of his larger mandibles, lifting upwards. There were sounds of spinning gears and cracking rocks. Hal's large red upper shoulders and arms, which were covered with fungi, separated from his body. He forcefully threw them away. His head was now on the top of his body, on a long neck that stretched above his lower—and now only—shoulders.

Mariska heard more gears whirling and more rocks cracking. Hal jumped forward, leaving the lower half of his large, heavy, 'Shroom laden, legs behind.

Hallvarður was no longer bulky and massive. Now he was just over two metres tall. With only two arms. He was more elegant looking, but still thick, like a tall, muscle-bound human man.

"Whoa!" shouted Mariska, "I didn't know you could do that."

"Oh, yeah, just another one of my many talents," he winked, "I needed to get rid of those vile growths. They were slowin' me down."

Now he'll definitely fit in my ship, thought Mariska, *one less problem to figure out.*

Mariska noticed that, luckily, the parts of his body that remained didn't have any fungal growths.

NAN-C, floating over their heads, interrupted: "There are many guard beasts coming toward us—in front and to the side."

Mariska was prepared as always. So she grabbed the tranq-gun from her pocket and took off running towards *Stellar Hermes* with Hallvarður close behind.

She saw one of the mushroom guards closing in front of her. Knowing she only had a limited number of tranquilliser blasts left, she knelt down and took careful aim, hitting the beast directly.

Just as she got up and continued running, another one jumped at Hal from the side. He knocked it out with a solid punch from his fist.

Hal threw another beast aside with an upthrust of ground.

Mariska was stressed, knowing that a beast could jump at her at any moment. She felt anxious not being in control of the situation. But she kept running forward. She turned the corner around a pile of junk and was knocked over by a mushroom beast.

Hal rounded the corner after her and a second beast lunged at him. He swung his powerful arm and missed.

The beast knocked him over.

Mariska easily tranquilized the creature on top of her, careful that it didn't fall directly onto her this time. She pushed it off, then jumped and spun, firing a tranq-blast at the beast pinning Hal and missing by half a metre.

Yeah, that was too fancy, she thought.

The beast spun its head towards her. She took more careful aim with the pistol, and just as it was about to pounce, she hit it directly. The beast fell to the ground unconscious.

"*Friendly*, aren't they!" yelled Mariska.

Hallvarður replied with a cocked eye.

They both took off running again, while NAN-C spouted directions from over their heads: "Straight... right... straight," leading them back to *Stellar Hermes*.

They encountered a couple more mushroom beasts on their way back, but not as many as Mariska had expected. As they rounded the last jumble of junk, Mariska suddenly understood why: six beasts were guarding *Stellar Hermes*.

She looked quickly at her tranq-pistol. She had two blasts left. "How are we going to get past all those?" asked Mariska.

"Maybe we can distra—"

But, NAN-C was already executing a plan. The orb had darted away from them and around another pile of garbage, where the orb's speakers started to make different loud sounds. A couple of the guards took off towards the flying computer.

Mariska took advantage of the situation and tranq-blasted two of the remaining beasts.

Hal rushed in and knocked the other two quickly unconscious by smacking their heads together.

Mariska ran to *Stellar Hermes*, opened the hatch and burst up the ramp. Hallvarður followed her up, ducking a little to fit through the hatchway. She quickly closed and locked the ramp behind him.

Casting her backpack on the bed, Mariska sat down in her pilot's chair and started to warm up *Stellar Hermes*. She wasn't worried about NAN-C, the orb would get back in a minute.

Hal came into the cockpit while she was finishing off the pre-flight checks and carefully sat down in the co-pilot's seat. It was almost too small for him, but he made it work.

The top hatch opened and NAN-C dropped inside, with the hatch sliding closed behind.

Stellar Hermes was ready to take off, so Mariska launcher her ship into the air, testing to make sure the recently added ionizer was flowing properly.

Mariska loved *Stellar Hermes*. It was a dream to fly, fast, agile, well built, and reliable. Her heart was racing now that she was in the cockpit of her ship again.

The ship was slowly climbing upwards—but still only fifty or sixty metres off the ground. Mariska was paying close attention to all the displays, making sure nothing went wrong—

The ship shook hard. Mariska looked at the sensors—there were objects flying all around them.

The ship rocked again. And again. Hal roared: "They're launching solid-state puffballs at us; those things have taken out lots of our ships!"

Enough with the testing, thought Mariska, and she pulled back on *Stellar Hermes's* yoke, thrusting it upwards—

But the ship didn't climb, it wouldn't go any higher. *Frak! The ionizer must be clogged!*

"Take the controls," barked Mariska, as she dove out of the pilot's seat, back towards the engine room to fix the ionizer.

"Uh…" called Hal, but it was too late; Mariska was too far away. She knew his flying skills weren't great, but if he could just keep them airborne and moving for a few minutes, it would be enough.

Mariska ran through the hatch to the engine room. She could feel *Stellar Hermes* tilting and swaying as Hal tried to evade the flying mushrooms.

The ship shook and lurched with hits from the puffballs. Mariska was straining as she tried hard not to lose her balance.

She brought up the flow readout on the nearby computer terminal and looked at the different ionic flows trying to determine which was clogged.

The ship dropped—

Mariska was launched upwards, then slammed down onto to the floor. She looked out the engine room hatch, through the length of her ship, and out the front windows—nothing but rock walls! She cursed Hal. *He must have flown us over the side of the canyon.* Stellar Hermes *would have dropped to the bottom of the ravine.*

The ship shook again with more shots of the solid-state puffballs.

"Yes!" screamed Mariska, as she found the block in the ionizer. She twirled some dials and flicked some switches on the ionizer and the clog started to dissipate. *It'll still take a couple minutes before we can get full height and thrust.*

As Mariska plopped down into the pilot's seat, she said in a mocking voice: "The canyon, Hal!? *Probably* not the best idea."

"Yeah, sorry about that; I'm not great at this evasive manoeuvring stuff."

Mariska took over the controls in just enough time to roll *Stellar Hermes* into another ravine, narrowly avoiding a looming wall. She pitched up again but didn't get much further away from the ground. So she thrust forward, hoping to lose a few of the mushroom ships in the canyon.

Mariska banked to the right, hugging tighter to the canyon wall than she felt was safe, hoping to take out some of the mushroom flyers.

It didn't work. The mushroom flyers were still after her—shooting more of the puffballs, which banged off *Stellar Hermes's* hull.

She noticed a higher section of the canyon floor, and she knew *Stellar Hermes* could clear it. She hoped it could be another chance to get rid of a few of the mushroom flyers. She dove her ship to the canyon bed, entirely too close for her own liking, and sped up.

At the last second she pitched her ship and tore upwards. This one worked! A couple of the mushroom flyers slammed into the wall.

Mariska tried to raise the ship higher off the ground but again she didn't gain much altitude. *The flow must still be partially clogged.*

Stellar Hermes was blazing through the canyon under Mariska's talented touch. Yawing right, banking left, pitching downward, spiralling upward. Mariska was in her element: flying.

Though the pursuit was dangerous and tense, Mariska was having the time of her life—these were the sorts of adventures she dreamed of having as a freelance courier. She whooped in excitement as she banked hard left to avoid a massive boulder.

She was completely in the zone, in total concentration, nothing could disturb her from the task.

A few kilometres in front was a mess of stalagmites. Mariska blasted *Stellar Hermes* towards them, planning to weave through the rock formations.

She quickly banked right around a spire, then rapidly left again, losing yet another mushroom flyer. Another left, another right, another right—she twisted her way through the maze of stalagmites with confidence.

She managed to take out a couple more mushroom flyers, but it wasn't enough. They were still pounding the ship with solid-state puffballs. *There's going to be so many new dents on poor* Hermes, thought Mariska.

Up ahead she noticed a "Y" in the canyon. She thought she'd try a tricky manoeuvre: wait until the last second before choosing a direction.

She waited…

And waited…

Her heart was racing…

And she chose left—

It was the wrong choice—a dead end.

There wasn't enough room to turn around, and stopping wasn't an option with all the flyers in close pursuit. So Mariska pulled hard on the yoke, hoping the clog was gone, hoping to fly over the top of the canyon wall.

Nothing happened. But she was determined, she was

not going to crash into that wall.

"Mariska!" yelled Hal from beside her, but she couldn't hear him in her intense concentration.

She continued to pull on the yoke—

Then suddenly, *Stellar Hermes* jerked forward and upward, blasting the comrades out of the canyon and up into the atmosphere. Leaving the mushrooms behind in their dust.

Part 2

Saving Minerallia

The two companions, Mariska Arisia and Rhodochrosite Tetrahedrite Quartz Hallvarður, had just daringly escaped from the mushroom planet Mycota, aboard the starship *Stellar Hermes*. Now they were hurtling towards Hal's home world: Minerallia.

Chapter 9

Minutes of Minerallia

Mariska was confidently piloting her starship as it streaked towards the nearby moon, Minerallia. Hal and Mariska both sat silently for a few minutes absorbing the action that they had just engaged in. Both were still a little anxious and slightly on guard.

While Mariska was pleased with her flying skills in the canyon, she was still completely focussed on her mission to quickly drop Hal off at home, then fly off to the Terrack-Pycon Ship Yards, and *finally* deliver her cargo.

She didn't want to let her client, Zefram Teeg, down. It was important to her to honour her social contract with Teeg and deliver his cargo—and she was getting *so* close.

Mariska could now see how close the moon was to

Mycota— Minerallia's orbit was clearly decayed beyond repair. Hal was staring at it and the sight of his home world seemed to trigger something deep inside him.

Hal, turning towards her from the neighbouring seat, reluctantly broke their silence, in his deep, gravelly voice: "Mariska... I wanted to ask you about your cargo. I noticed it when it fell out from your bag in the forest." His voice was slow and controlled and it seemed that he was having trouble saying what he wanted to say. Maybe he was choosing his words carefully or maybe he was afraid. Mariska didn't know.

Hallvarður continued, with a little more conviction and passion: "I recognize the shape of it. I think it means something to my people. I have a feeling that it can help save Minerallia."

Mariska continued in her silence—she was worried that she knew exactly where this conversation was going.

"I don't..." stammered Hal, "really know what the artifact does. But I definitely remember seeing that same shape in the ancient Minerallian city.

"I remember it being on an old wall mural with other images of moons and structures. I think it's important to my people. I believe it can save us!

"I was hoping that, maybe, you could help me save Minerallia."

"Help you save Minerallia!?" responded Mariska, "I'm

only one person; I can't do anything about a moon that's losing its orbit! I have to deliver the cargo to my client. I really have to drop you off quickly. I'm already late and I have a contract to uphold."

The conversation went exactly where Mariska worried it would go, but she tried to remain calm, keeping her emotions suppressed. Hal was getting noticeably—and understandably—worked up about his situation.

Hal continued to plead: "I... I know that you're an honourable person... but *we* need your help. The cargo is nothing more than a pretty trinket to your client."

"How do you know what it is to my client!?" retorted Mariska, and she immediately regretted saying it.

"I'm sure it can save my planet. I told you, I recognize it. I know that it can save my people! And I'm going to save them even if they don't want to save themselves!" He was starting to get really agitated. His emotions were pouring out of him.

Mariska was worried he might burst into tears. The thought of it made her feel flustered. Emotional outbursts were not something she was equipped to deal with—and hysterical crying was the worst.

Taking a deep breath, and slowly turning to look in Hallvarður's eyes, she said: "I'm sorry, Hal. I just can't give you someone else's property. He entrusted me to deliver it—and that's what I'm going to do." Mariska snapped her head around in a motion that clearly meant: *this conversation is over.*

But Hal wasn't done, he continued in a louder voice: "Mariska, please. I know that it can save my people. We may not have much time left, we don't know when Minerallia will finally crash into Mycota. It could be tomorrow!"

Hallvarður took a deep breath, looked downwards, and in a quieter voice he added: "How can you have the deaths of an entire species on your conscience?"

People die every day, thought Mariska. If she stopped to help every life form that was in distress, where would she be!?

"It's just some cargo," continued Hal, "it's not worth anything compared to the life of thousands of people!"

She sat in silence for a few more moments with Hal looking beseechingly at her. Mariska shook her head slowly, and finally, in a quiet voice, almost a whisper, Mariska spoke: "I can't, Hal. I just can't." She punctuated it with sigh.

Hallvarður huffed in frustration. But when Mariska set her mind to something, the only thing that could change it, was her.

The rest of the short trip to Minerallia was silent except for the sounds of the working starship. Hallvarður was trying to use his calming routine to quiet his temper. Mariska was piloting her ship, trying to ignore the thoughts reeling through her mind.

I wish we would get to Minerallia faster.
I wish that I wasn't so late for the delivery.
I wish Hal hadn't asked me to give up the cargo.
I just want to be alone.

She didn't usually let other people onto *Stellar Hermes*— but this time it was necessary. Her ship—her home—was a sanctuary for her, to escape the noise and pressure of other beings. It was her private oasis and having another creature inside was invasive. She wouldn't be able to feel completely comfortable again for a few days after he'd gone. Other people left an aura in the space and it took some time to dissipate.

Mariska was getting stressed. She took a few deep breaths, pushing out her chest, trying to abate the feeling.

She was happy to save Hal's life, but the cargo wasn't hers to give—she had to deliver it to her client.

. . .

The duo finally reached Minerallia and Mariska landed *Stellar Hermes* where Hal asked her to.

Hallvarður stepped into the airlock, and turned to her, saying: "Mariska, thank you for saving my life on the 'Shroom planet." Then his face turned a little more serious and he pleaded: "But, please reconsider. You can help my people—you can help *me!*"

Mariska looked at him for a moment, then quietly responded: "I can't, Hal... I just can't. I'm sorry... Good-bye, Hal." He nodded and turned around as Mariska closed the inner hatch.

Mariska watched Hal walk off the end of the landing ramp and out into the atmosphere-less, rock-laden ground of Minerallia. Hallvarður didn't look back. From his gait, Mariska realized he felt dejected.

She closed up the landing ramp—and she was alone again. Mariska sighed deeply. She powered up her starship's engines and blasted off for the Terrack-Pycon Ship Yards. It was time to deliver her cargo.

Chapter 10

Conveyance of Cargo

Mariska's thoughts were in turmoil; she couldn't stop thinking about what Hal had asked of her. She silently sat in the pilot's seat—exhausted—while *Stellar Hermes* shot, on autopilot, towards the Terrack-Pycon Ship Yards.

It was in the late night hours at the station and there was no point getting there until morning. She was already late and Zefram Teeg never conducted business outside of regular working hours. So she was taking the slow route.

It would give her plenty of time to think and she was completely alone now, so she could really concentrate in the silence.

Mariska stared out the windows at the vastness of

space before her—the distant suns helped her relax and focus. She noticed the patterns of constellations, tilting her head left and right, blinking her eyes open and closed, lining up different stars with the edges of the windows.

Only half paying attention, she looked down at the control board and made a few minor corrections to the course, letting her reflexes make the judgements. Her mind was too full with other thoughts to be fully distracted by something a computer could do competently.

Mariska left the cockpit and disrobed, taking off her dirty clothes and chucking them in the washer. She climbed into the shower and let the warmth help her thoughts flow. The fact that it was doubly cut off from the outside world gave her the extra seclusion she needed to really engage with her thoughts. And because it was such a small space, it felt like the thoughts just bounced off the walls and back again, allowing her to focus and rebound ideas.

Was Hal just being overly emotional about Minerallia? She sometimes couldn't distinguish between honest emotions and hysterics.

Is the moon really going to be destroyed so soon? It was definitely low in orbit, but she was no physicist.

Should I give my cargo to Hal? No. She had to deliver the cargo or it would be stealing.

Will I regret not helping Hal? Would she regret not

honouring her contract with Zefram Teeg?

What will Zefram Teeg think of me if I don't deliver his cargo? What would Hal think of her if she didn't help him?

Mariska stood in the shower, letting the water bead over her body, letting the warmth envelope her, letting her fingers and toes shrivel. Finally, she left the steamy warmth.

She donned a light tunic and walked to the kitchenette. She made sure the floor of *Stellar Hermes* was always heated so that it was warm enough to walk around in bare feet. It was her home after all and she didn't want to have to wear boots all the time.

Mariska suddenly realized that she had become ravenously hungry. In fact she was feeling a little weak. Rummaging through her fridge and cupboards, she picked out some vegetables and leftover, white, sticky rice to make a stir fry. She wasn't really in the mood to make decisions, so she chose an easy option.

Mariska stood over the stove stirring the vegetables but she couldn't fully concentrate on cooking.

She knew that she had to get to the ship yards.

She knew that she had to deliver the cargo.

It was important for her to honour her contract with her client.

But it was also important to help Hal—he too needed

her. And his people may become extinct.

Was work—and her reputation—more important than a whole species of alien life?

Is my business relationship with Teeg more important than my friendship with Hal?

Mariska knew that often, it was better to let her subconscious figure things out while she slept. She'd heard that your subconscious already knew the answer to your thoughts and questions, it just took time for your conscious brain to become aware of that information. Maybe that's what gut feelings were: your subconscious hinting at the right choice, telling your body what direction to go.

After eating her supper, which was delicious, although most people would say it was bland, Mariska double checked the autopilot computer, shut out all the interior lights in *Stellar Hermes*, and dropped into bed. Usually she would read a couple of chapters from her favourite adventure novel, but she didn't feel up to it tonight.

Mariska laid her head down on her pillow, making sure it was centred and straight. She sealed the blankets snuggly all around her body to keep in all the warmth.

Mariska worried that maybe her brain would keep her awake, but the physical—and mental—exertion of the whole day took precedence, and, almost instantly, she fell asleep.

Mariska awoke early. She had programmed *Stellar Hermes* to slowly increase the light intensity onboard to simulate dawn on a planet. Like any other day, she jumped into the shower. This day was going to be very different: she was going to talk with Zefram Teeg. He always made her a little nervous with his unpredictability.

After getting out of the shower, Mariska got dressed, readying herself to deliver her cargo. She hadn't yet thought about Hal today. She felt completely alone in her ship and that was a good thing. She should have felt some residual effects of having another person around the day before, but there were none. It confused her for a second and she stopped moving.

She'd only felt the aura dissipate so quickly a few times before, with her previous best friends. She always felt so comfortable around them, she didn't feel the social pressure and she was QX with being quiet. But they both had disappeared from her life without warning. She had thought that maybe it was her introversion that turned them away. Though she felt comfortable in silence, she believed they never did. At least that's what she rationalized herself into believing. She gave up on finding new friends because she was happy alone—and nobody had ever *felt* right.

But Hallvarður did.

Mariska stood in the middle of the floor, frozen in the midst of drying her hair, when her conscious mind clicked with the information her subconscious had known for hours: she needed to save Hal.

Immediately a plan popped into her head. A plan that was just waiting in her subconsciousness for her brain to catch up: she would deliver her cargo to Teeg, as per her contract, then buy it back from him to help save Hal.

A sense of dread dropped into her stomach: she would have to bargain with Teeg. It was something she'd hoped she would never have to do—he was ruthless. Mariska started second guessing her decisions, as she always did. Doubt floated into her mind:

Is this really the best idea?

Maybe I could just avoid talking to Zefram Teeg.

Maybe Hal will be safe without me.

The thoughts twirled around for a few seconds then Mariska snapped out of it: *No, I have to face him. The plan is good. This is what I need to do!*

Mariska jumped back into motion with a new sense of energy and a renewed happiness. She knew this was the right thing to do, this was the thing that made her feel completely at ease.

Hal is my friend. I want to save him.

A new sense of desperation crept over her as she realized that a whole species could have died with her inaction.

First she had to see if she could actually afford the artifact. She needed to check her untouchable savings to see how much she had available. The money was for absolute emergencies only—like a new ionizer—but this situation seemed to qualify. "NAN-C, how much is available in my savings account?"

"Good morning, dear," responded NAN-C, cooing with motherly love, "last time I synchronized with the banking systems, there was nine-thousand two-hundred fifty-eight credits."

Hopefully I can make that work, thought Mariska, subconsciously knowing that the cargo was worth more. She'd have to hold some of her credits back, in case of emergency repairs, but seven-thousand should be enough for the artifact.

Maybe Teeg will still pay me some for the delivery, even though it's so late. Not that her delivery fee was high enough to help much with the purchase of the artifact.

Mariska finished getting ready for the day. She put on more formal attire for her meeting with Teeg, ate some breakfast, and settled into the pilot's seat for the final approach to the Terrack-Pycon Ship Yards.

Chapter 11

Tyranny of Teeg

The Terrak-Pycon Ship Yards loomed ahead. It was constructed of two oblong asteroids that were held together by human and alien engineering. A hodgepodge of odd looking structures snaked around, penetrated from, and gouged into the two asteroids. It was now more structure than asteroid, and home to thousands of creatures performing legal—and illegal—activities.

It wasn't Mariska's favourite place to be, but some of her rich, eccentric clients, that paid really well, lived here—Zefram Teeg was one of those clients.

After following the docking procedures, Mariska stayed in her starship for a couple of minutes, mentally preparing for the confrontation with Teeg. He was really unpredictable. It was like there were two people in him: a nice, helpful, old man; and a vile, angry, geezer. And he seemed to swing between them with each sentence he spoke, without anybody knowing which version of him would come out.

Mariska stowed the cargo box in a nice satchel, to be presentable for Teeg, and started to make her way through the dingy hallways of the ship yards.

The halls were dark and dusty, with ominous shadows in every corner that hinted at the unpleasant beings that roamed around. And it stunk: a putrid, rotting smell of the body odour of countless creatures, of burnt skin from laser blasts, and of machine oil. Mariska's nose curled and flared involuntarily—her sense of smell was hypersensitive at the best of times, so this was overwhelming.

She kept her head down, not wanting to interact with anybody. She just wanted to get to Teeg and get this conversation over with—and the sooner the better. She whisked past raucous bars with groaning ogres; brightly lit emporiums of questionable merchandise; and blinking game saloons with sultry, semi-honest, male and female companions.

Finally reaching the level that was Teeg's, Mariska got really nervous, with cold sweats and imperceptible twitches. At least this section of the ship yards was clean and bright and well maintained—Teeg wouldn't have it any other way.

She walked up to the receptionist and asked to meet Zefram Teeg. The android, because Teeg wouldn't trust a living being with his important secrets, motioned for Mariska to sit and wait. Sitting and waiting only made her more anxious, she was tapping her foot, and darting her eyes around uncomfortably, while tightly holding the cargo on her lap.

Mariska was finally allowed to enter Teeg's lavish office, full of countless artifacts of unknown origins. *This is going to be a hard bargain*, thought Mariska. The walls were at least six metres high, covered with shelves filled to the brim. Directly in front of her was a wall of windows that showed the outline of the pinkish gas giant they were orbiting. Directly in the centre was a large desk made completely of gem-encrusted stone.

Behind the desk was the short, rotund man, dressed in a thick, wool-like, highly tailored suit coat, with a bizarre pattern of greys, greens, and bronzes. The lapels and cuffs were deep gold and punctuated with golden clasps. He was seated in a large throne, leaning menacingly forward on his desk, looking directly at Mariska with his pudgy face, nasty smirk, and deep-set, brown eyes.

She put on her confident face and strolled in to greet Zefram Teeg.

"Ms. Arisia," Teeg started firmly, the vile personality appearing, "I've been waiting for you; I expected you to get here days ago."

"Yes, I had a couple of... complications," replied Mariska. The less information she gave him the better. And she never called him sir like other people did—he didn't deserve the honour.

"You still have *my* shipment?" he said, still crotchety.

"Yes, it's here."

"Good," he responded in a more jovial tone, "I'm willing to let the lateness slide because of your previous outstanding work." Then he punctuated it with a gruff: "Hand it over."

Mariska placed the artifact on his desk, and hoped this confrontation would be easy—but she knew it wouldn't be. She would have much preferred to interact via interstellar text message, but that wasn't how Teeg operated.

He stood, held up the artifact, and examined it.

This was the first time Mariska had actually looked at the cargo. It was brilliant. A generally circular object that you could hold in one hand, with seven protrusions around the outside, of varying thicknesses and lengths. There was a large, central, jade gemstone, surrounded by a circle of silver, and another circle of solid granite. The protrusions were capped with different rocks and minerals: red sandstone, obsidian, quartz, pink fluorite, platinum, beryl, and strontianite.

She took a deep breath as she fully realized: *it belonged to Minerallia.*

Teeg, still staring at the rock object, said: "This is a great addition to my collection, don't you think Ms. Arisia?"

Mariska was staring at the object and jolted to attention when he spoke. She looked at Teeg, and with her most confident voice, said: "I wanted to talk to you about that."

"Hmm..." he responded absently.

Mariska continued, hoping the angry Teeg wouldn't come forward: "I... would like to buy it from you."

"Is that so. How much is it worth to you?" Mariska knew that Teeg was always willing to make a profit, he'd sell his own brother if it was opportune. But his tone was disinterested and calm.

Mariska tried a low number first, wanting to keep some of her hard earned money, yet, hoping he wouldn't get upset, and that she could deal with the nice Teeg. "I'll give you five-thousand credits."

"Five-thousand!" *That* was the angry Teeg. He stopped admiring his possession and looked towards her, saying: "I could easily sell this for much more; it is worth it. But I wouldn't because it has a certain sentimental value to me."

On guard now, she increased her bid: "I'll give you seven-thousand," responded Mariska. That was the top of what she was willing to spend, she needed to keep some back for emergencies.

Zefram Teeg was silent, which was usually not a good sign, and that made Mariska even more worried. Not only did she have to talk to a mercurial human being, but she also had to bargain with him, both of which were extremely hard for her. And Hal was relying on her—she was desperate to help his people. The pressure was almost overwhelming, but she didn't want Teeg to know that. Sweat was dripping from her arm pits and her hands were damp and clammy. She needed to project her most confident self to Teeg; he ate fear for breakfast.

Teeg lifted his free arm into the air and motioned around the room at the shelves of artifacts. "There are plenty of other things I could sell you; a few of which may be within your budget," asserted Teeg.

He held the stone object with two hands and looked down at it and added: "I've just recently grown quite attached to this item. It deserves a place in my wondrous collection."

Starting to really feel the pressure, Mariska sweetened her deal: "I'll wave my delivery fee for this job," and trying to play his game, whether it would work or not, she added: "as a gesture of our continued friendship."

"You think I was going to pay your delivery fee after you're days late?" barked the vile Teeg. Then he stood there silently, and Mariska knew he was waiting for her to respond.

"Yes." She almost added, "I was hoping so," but thought maybe that would show her hand too soon.

"Hmm... For what you're offering I can give you my Semian Gemstone on the third shelf there. It's a marvellous piece."

Mariska realized that he was playing her, trying to get as much money as he could. His game was transparent, he didn't really care for the Minerallian item any more than the other objects in his collection—which was to say he cared only as much as his profit. But, to Mariska, it seemed like she had no other option than making her bid higher—even if it meant spending everything.

She knew she had to risk it all for Hallvarður.

"All I have is nine-thousand two-hundred, Teeg," declared Mariska. She was so worried, she had nothing else to offer him and this was every last credit she owned. In an instant of weakness, she quietly added: "Please." And she immediately regretted showing emotion in his presence.

Zefram Teeg stared into her eyes for a moment, then blinked slowly. Maybe he saw a hint of her desperation. Maybe it was the nice side of Teeg. But, he agreed: "Fine. But you owe me a few deliveries—no questions asked."

Mariska didn't like owing people things, but she

knew she wouldn't get a better deal. So she nodded in acceptance and said thank you. They shook hands. She gathered the artifact and left Teeg's office at a very brisk pace. She continued her speed walking all the way back to *Stellar Hermes* and launched as soon as they would let her go.

She was ready to help Hal.

Chapter 12

Grotto of Gems

Stellar Hermes flew at full speed back to Minerallia, this time through hyperspace—Mariska didn't want to waste any more time. When she approached Minerallia, it had fallen even lower in orbit—their fate reseted squarely on Mariska's shoulders. Yet, even with the enormous pressure, she was excited at the prospect of seeing Hal again.

Her last visit to the small moon was very quick and she didn't get a chance to really see what she was trying to save. Mariska hoped that she would get ample opportunity to appreciate the ancient Minerallian craftsmanship after this adventure was over.

But she was extremely worried she would fail.

Mariska landed her ship at the same coordinates as the last time, when she dropped Hallvarður off. Knowing that the moon had no atmosphere, Mariska donned her sleek space suit, and started to exit *Stellar Hermes*. The gravity was very low, making her lanky walk even more clumsy looking—like a stick-bug trying ballet.

Reaching the bottom of the landing ramp, she noticed a Minerallian was approaching her—it wasn't Hal. Mariska's heart dropped a little, she was really hoping Hal would be here to greet her. Mariska wanted Hallvarður to know she didn't abandon him, she wanted his approval.

This new rock giant was completely different from Hallvarður: slender and tall, with two arms and two legs. Where human muscles would have been, there were rough, green spheroids. Its knees, elbows, and shoulders were punctuated with amber blocks, and at the top of its head was a series of tall protrusions of the same amber mineral. Everything was connected together with a black stone. As the giant elegantly drifted towards Mariska she wished she could move her lengthy body that smoothly.

The rock person approached Mariska and started to speak. The giant's mouth moved, but the sound didn't come from its mouth, there was no atmosphere to propel it. The sound emanated up from the ground, through Mariska's space boots. It was an unusual sensation, she could see its mouth move, then a moment later, hear the words vibrating up through her spacesuit. It must have been another of the Minerallian's powers, part of their connection with the rocks, stones and ground.

The rock giant's voice was slow and even. "Welcome Mariska Arisia. I'm Wulfenite Mimetite Smoky Quartz Dagbjartur." She paused for a moment, only reminding Mariska of the slowness of her words, then continued: "Rhodochrosite Tetrahedrite Quartz Hallvarður left a message for you before he departed," and another long pause. "His words were exactly: 'I knew you'd come back. You found me once before and you can find me again.'" Then the creature with the dull personality turned and started to stride away from Mariska.

Mariska was going to call out and ask more questions— she had so many things she wanted to know about the people and about Hallvarður. But she knew it would be futile without an atmosphere to transmit her sound waves. She boarded *Stellar Hermes* and contemplated Hal's message, while taking off her snug spacesuit.

Just as she was stowing her suit, the solution popped into her head: the cargo tagger. Hal must have left it attached to his chest so she could locate him. It's a good thing the cargo tagger used the Inter-Planetary Tracking Service satellite system—it would let her find Hallvarður accurately anywhere in the planetary system.

As Mariska was warming up *Stellar Hermes*, she asked

her trustworthy computer: "NAN-C, locate Hal."

"Hallvarður is in the southern hemisphere of Mycota. Over seven-hundred kilometres away from the area we have been previously."

Mycota, thought Mariska, *why would he go back there? He had mentioned going there before, but why now?* Mariska had to admit that the mystery of it all was a little intriguing—even with the pressure of saving the whole Minerallian species.

She launched her vessel and headed towards the coordinates on Mycota that NAN-C had plotted.

. . .

Mariska was feeling uneasy about going back to Mycota, primarily because of her last adventure on the planet. But more importantly, she was worried about what Hal would think of her. She wanted to prove to him that she was a good human being and that she cared about her friends.

Deep inside, Mariska knew that Hal accepted her and she *knew* that he understood her.

Descending through the lower atmosphere of Mycota, Mariska surmised that the large ruins ahead was her destination. And she was correct. The coordinates pointed her to the outskirts of a large crumbled city.

Even though the city was completely demolished and covered in fungi, Mariska saw that at one point in history it had been an awesome sight. Everything was made out of rocks, stones, and minerals; with beautiful colours of ruby, amber, yellow, emerald, lapis, indigo, and violet, glinting in the sunlight. There were huge structures that had fallen down, or toppled over. A couple of tall columns still stood on the land, pointing up to the heavens in defiance. There were also mounds of unknown structures, covered with grey lichen.

Wherever Mariska looked, there were different kinds of rocks; varying structures of minerals; unusual colours of gemstones—and everything was massive. A city for giant sentient rock beings.

With a renewed sense of excitement, Mariska strode towards the city. Off in the distance she saw a familiar shape standing and waiting for her: Hallvarður. She rushed up to him and words burst from her mouth: "I'm sorry, Hal."

"Not to worry, I've always had complete faith in you. I knew that you just needed some time alone to figure things out," he responded in a calm tone—yet he still had so much more personality than the Minerallian she had met earlier.

His words made Mariska blush a little. At that moment, she realized that he was a true friend.

Hal pointed behind her, up into the sky, and added in an excited voice: "But now I think we need to hurry."

Mariska turned around, looked up, and noticed Minerallia, high in the sky. Its orbit had decayed so much that it was a large glowing orb in the daytime sky.

"I'm glad you found me again," added Hal, as he removed the cargo tagger from his chest and threw it to the ground. "I have something I want to show you."

They walked off over a crumbled roadway towards a large sunken grotto. Everything was gigantic. Descending the immense steps, Mariska noticed what used to be a fountain made of deep grey stone in the centre. She looked up, and above them, over their heads now, was the fenced opening of the grotto, with golden posts and obsidian handles.

Hal lead her, around the fountain, to the left side of the grotto. Directly in front of the friends, was a wall of gems. In fact the grotto was circular, and *every* wall was covered in murals made from gemstones of countless varieties: onyx, amethyst, kornerupine, pyrope, azurite, aquamarine, celestine, pink sapphire, diamond, and more. It was a dazzling site even in the dim light.

"This is where I had seen the shape of your cargo before," said Hal, pointing to one of the large murals. Mariska immediately noticed the same shape as the artifact that she was carrying. She reached into her backpack and pulled it out to compare.

"What does it mean, Hal?"

"This is a mural of an ancient myth told to children. It's about Minerallia, before The Big Merge, before the Mycotazens. It shows our vast, ancient race of builders, and makers; a utopia.

"And here, in this illustration, it depicts moons surrounding what is now Mycota. But you'll notice the moons have a symbol on them, the symbol means protector.

"From the old story, my ancestors created these moons to protect our civilization, it was their greatest achievement of construction. And I believe the moon we now live on is one of The Protectors."

Mariska looked at the illustration of Mycota with three moons surrounding it, and asked: "What happened to the Minerallians?"

"I believe... The Big Merge happened. Somehow the Mycotazens got to our planet and destroyed our civilization. Maybe their spores came from The First System, maybe the environment changed to support their life. I don't really know."

Mariska noticed Hallvarður's excitement as he explained the murals to her, but she was still a little confused: "But how does my cargo help?"

"I believe it's a key. If you look over there it shows the

key being somehow attached to The Protector, at its north pole. And you can see the next illustration depicts the moon moving—on its own power."

Hal's voice was really excited and brimming with energy now. In what seemed like a conclusion, he added: "If we can get the key to the north pole of Minerallia, and activate The Protector, we can save my people."

Mariska knew that now was the time to act, so she looked into Hal's eyes and said: "QX; let's do it!"

Chapter 13

Satellites of Safety

The two friends blasted their way to Minerallia, and Mariska landed *Stellar Hermes* right next to the north pole. Mariska put on her spacesuit, a task she didn't enjoy, but she was happy to do it for Hal. Then they both exited *Stellar Hermes* to find the location for the key.

NAN-C, like always, bobbed beside them.

As soon as they descended the ramp, Hallvarður bent over and felt the ground. He touched his hands to the ground, stood up and said: "Now that I understand more about Minerallia, I can feel the difference in the ground. I can feel the structures of this moon."

Like the other rock giant Mariska had met on Minerallia, the sound of Hal's voice did not come from his mouth, but reverberated up through her boots to meet her ears. She could see his mouth move, but the sound was completely disconnected—it was a disconcerting sensation.

Mariska stood in silence and watched. Hal took a few steps forward and she felt the ground grumble and shake. *He must be using his powers*, thought Mariska.

Immediately in front of Hal, the ground opened up, revealing a ramp leading downwards into the moon. Hal motioned for Mariska to follow him as he started his descent.

Reaching the bottom of the ramp, a doorway opened into a large cavernous room made of dark grey rock. In the centre was a circular console, and on top stood a layered cylindrical cog. The cog was about a metre high with layers of different types of rocks and minerals, sprinkled with streaks of semi-transparent gems.

Directly facing the duo, on the sloped side of the console, was the keyhole. Mariska ran over to it and held up the key. The keyhole was inset into the console and had seven protrusions that exactly matched up with the key. At the tip of each was a matching mineral: red sandstone, obsidian, quartz, pink fluorite, platinum, beryl, and strontianite.

Mariska turned the key in her hands, orienting it to match the keyhole, then placed it in—

A greenish glow started around the central jade

gemstone of the key, then it began to radiate outwards through the key's teeth. As it hit the different minerals the colour changed to match the mineral's colour, and beams shot out of each protrusion along criss-crossing channels in the console. The coloured veins lit up the whole chamber as they snaked their way through the room.

Underneath the cylindrical cog, the glowing paths coalesced and seemed to energize the cog as the melded white light worked its way up the cog's sides. The cavern shuttered and rumbled and the cog began to turn counterclockwise—

Then stopped—

It lurched again as though it was trying to turn—but couldn't.

Mariska looked at Hal's disappointed face, then back at the cog. *What is stopping it?* she wondered. She didn't have to peer too closely at the cog to figure the problem out. She noticed a large crack severing the cog laterally—the white light stopped at that point and didn't extend up the length of the cog.

Mariska jumped onto the console, easily in the light gravity, pointed to the crack, and motioned to Hal. He moved closer, looking obviously upset, and said: "What should we do?"

Mariska shrugged her shoulders. Her brain, working

fast, came up with a solution: the other moon! They could get its cog and bring it back here. This was one of the *rare* instances where she wished she could talk.

"Hal," she tried, "we can get the cog from the other moon!" He just shook his head. He couldn't hear her, but saw her lips move.

She drew a circle in the air. Then pointed to the ground. Made the symbol for "two". Pointed up the ramp.

Hal just looked at her with a confused face, his head slightly tilted to the side. The hand motions weren't working.

Maybe NAN-C has an idea. Mariska was getting anxious, she needed to communicate with Hal. Mariska spoke into her helmet: "NAN-C, how can I get my sound to Hal?" Talking to NAN-C worked without atmosphere because her suit's intercom was connected wirelessly with NAN-C.

"I have no conclusive ideas, hon," responded NAN-C.

"Could you attach yourself to Hal, and project my voice through your speaker? Maybe my voice will vibrate within Hal's body like his vibrates in the ground."

"Your theory is reasonable. I shall try."

During the conversation, Hal was getting agitated, probably because he felt like he was missing something.

NAN-C darted over to Hallvarður's shoulder and clamped on.

NAN-C relayed back: "Try now, dear."

"Hal!" yelled Mariska.

He responded: "Yes! I can hear you. Your voice is vibrating through my body, just like mine must vibrate through yours."

"That was the plan," Mariska responded excitedly. "I have an idea. This cog is broken, but we can jet over to the other moon and grab its cog and bring it back here."

"That just might work!"

Mariska grabbed the key from the keyhole—she didn't want to leave something so important behind. The three of them darted back up the ramp, ran back to the surface of Minerallia, and boarded *Stellar Hermes*.

Mariska only removed her helmet, keeping the rest of her spacesuit on, because she knew she'd need it again as soon as they landed on the next moon.

Mariska dropped into the pilot's chair, ignited *Stellar Hermes's* engines, and blasted them off towards the other moon.

. . .

Stellar Hermes shot towards the other—significantly larger—moon, and again, landed at the north pole. Mariska replaced her helmet and the two adventurers darted down the landing ramp.

Hal, with NAN-C still clamped to his shoulder, came to a quick stop at the bottom. He briskly bent over and started caressing the ground. His motions became frantic. He jumped to another spot and felt again. Mariska could feel frustration emanating from him. She could hear grunts and huffs coming up through her boots.

"What is it?" Mariska asked.

"This moon has no structure. It's not like Minerallia. It's not artificial; it's a completely natural body!"

"Uh. QX, lets go to the third moon then."

"There is no third moon!" yelled Hallvarður.

"The mural you showed me had three moons: one larger, this one; and two smaller moons with the symbols on them."

"But there are only two moons of Mycota."

"The illustration showed three," responded Mariska. She knew she was right, but Hal didn't believe her. "NAN-C, did you take an image of the mural?"

"Of course, love. As you know, I record everything," cooed NAN-C.

"Project the mural so we can look at it."

One of the knobs on the side of the spherical computer's body lit up, and a blueish image of the mural was projected over the ground. Mariska pointed the three moons out to Hal, then asked: "Where's the third one? It must be the other Protector."

"I don't know. For my whole life, there have only been two moons," responded Hal, in an angry, yet disappointed voice.

Mariska knew that he was too upset to think of a solution to this problem—he was worrying about his people. But she was energized and aware. She knew he was relying on her, so she probed for ideas: "This mural was created before The Big Merge?"

"Yes."

"So, at one point, there were three moons..." and Mariska trailed off into thought. She knew that there were lots of planetary bodies in the system with eccentric orbits, and some of the planetoids intermixed between the two systems. "NAN-C, could a moon have broken orbit from Mycota during The Big Merge?"

"Yes; it is possible."

Where is the most likely location for the moon, thought Mariska as Hal slammed his fists to the ground and bent over in frustration.

"NAN-C, display the planetary system diagram." NAN-C complied and the projection switched to a star chart. Mariska looked around the diagram. The moon they were currently on was highlighted green, and the rest of the combined systems rotated around them in glowing blue. They were in the outer rim of the First System, where The Old System orbited. The next closest planet further in system was Vandia, which Terrack-Pycon orbited. Between that planet and The Old System was only the asteroid belt.

Mariska's mind was reeling with ideas and she started asking NAN-C questions: "Does the third planet in The Old System have any moons?"

"No."

"Does Vandia?"

"Vandia is orbited by the Terrack-Pycon Ship Yards, but no spherical planetoids."

"What about the asteroid belt; could the moon have been sucked into it?"

"That is plausible."

QX; that's a lead, mused Mariska. Trying to figure out what to do next, she asked: "NAN-C are there bodies from both merged systems in the asteroid belt?"

"Yes, dear."

"Can you display only the bodies from The Old System?"

"Yes, that information is in my databanks thanks to the Outer Rim Stellar Cartography Project."

The projection on the ground flashed and everything except bodies believed to belong to The Old System faded to a darker blue. "Now, are there any asteroids the same size as Minerallia?" asked Mariska.

"One moment... Yes. There is a single planetoid with the same mean radius and gross mass as Minerallia."

Perfect, thought Mariska. Then she bounded over to Hal and placed her hand on his sunken, dejected shoulder. "Hal, I know where the other moon is. It's in the asteroid belt! NAN-C has located it for us."

"Really!?" responded Hallvarður as he looked up into her eyes expectantly.

Mariska was about to respond, when something caught her eye—

There in the sky, above horizon, off in the distance, Mariska saw that edge of Minerallia glowing; it's orbit had completely decayed and it was burning up as it entered the outer atmosphere of Mycota.

"No time to talk!" she yelled and bounded towards *Stellar Hermes*. Hal's head jerked to the side as he also noticed the sinking ball of fire. He stood up and ran after Mariska.

As Mariska was ascending the landing ramp she called out: "NAN-C how much time until Minerallia completely crashes?"

"I estimate less than two hours," responded NAN-C.

Just as Hal shut the inner airlock, Mariska blasted off, not waiting for him to settle.

Mariska's mind was whirling as they shot off towards the missing moon. Two hours wasn't going to be enough time to get to the asteroid belt and back—especially with all the space pirates.

Chapter 14

Area of Asteroids

Stellar Hermes was in hyperspace; Mariska was trying to get as close to the belt, as fast as she could. She'd have to drop out of hyperspace to navigate the asteroid belt—it was a cluttered mess of rocks and ice.

"So, there's still a chance!?" asked Hal.

"Yeah, we just have to get there and back in one piece," responded Mariska. She was worried it was going to be a lot harder than she wanted it to be.

That was the extent of their conversation for the three-quarters of an hour. Mariska had nothing to add and Hallvarður needed the silence to remain calm.

Stellar Hermes dropped out of hyperspace with the asteroid belt looming in front of them. Mariska was in the zone now as she began to pilot her star cruiser through the cluster of rocks and ice.

This asteroid belt defied all space physics—it was a tight knot of matter. An unpredictable mash of rock and ice, of dust, planetoids, and everything in between. Not only were the asteroids orbiting statically, quite often they shifted and moved, crashing into each other and sending chunks flying.

It was a complete nightmare to navigate—and that's why the space pirates loved it. They could hide here and nobody would bother them.

But Mariska had flown it before, so she knew what to expect.

Mariska was rolling around asteroids, and pitching over ice balls. *Stellar Hermes* narrowly missed the collision of two ice balls as Mariska boldly piloted her ship underneath the wreckage.

An oblong potato shaped rock spun towards the star cruiser, narrowly missing them. Out of the corner of her eye, Mariska saw Hal cringe but she wasn't worried.

A blip sounded on the scanners, announcing the approach of a space vessel. Mariska tucked *Stellar Hermes* tight beside an asteroid, hoping the pirate pilot wasn't paying as much attention as she was. Thankfully the ship just passed slowly by.

They continued their dangerous passage through the

array of rocks. Hallvarður pointed out a ship wreck off their port side. Mariska noticed a rogue satellite floating above them. Everywhere they looked was a spinning, changing, imposing mass of rock and ice. Both of their eyes were darting up, down, left, right: Mariska's eyes plotting her course, Hallvarður's eyes twitching in fright.

The passage was treacherous, but the companions finally came to what looked like a large spherical clearing in the asteroid belt. Directly in the centre was the moon they were looking for: the final Protector.

Unfortunately, there was lots of activity on the scanner around the planetoid, and that meant lots of space pirates.

On the equator, facing towards them, was a large, city-sized fortress not unlike Terrack-Pycon. It was a mishmash of random pieces, broken ship hulls, cargo containers, and random bubbles of metal. It looked fatigued and frightful—not a place any sane being would live. But the pirates weren't sane.

Mariska let out a sigh of distress, and Hal agreed with his own grunt, adding: "How are we going to get through that?"

"At least it looks like there aren't any at the north pole," responded Mariska in an overly optimistic tone.

She pitched her starship upwards and moved along the inside edge of the clearing in the asteroid belt. She decided to drop down to the moon from the top of the clearing, since most of the ships were located laterally around the equator. Maybe they wouldn't notice her coming down from the top—but she didn't have high hopes for the situation.

And the time restriction wasn't helping. It had taken them another twenty minutes to get this far—that left less than an hour for Minerallia.

How many other vessels have tried to sneak up on a space pirate fortress and lived to tell about it? Mariska was hoping *lots*, but she suspected otherwise.

They approached the top of the moon and were looking out the forward windows towards it. They couldn't see any activity around the pole, but that didn't ease Mariska's mind. As soon as she left the protection of the asteroid cluster, and approached the moon, the pirates were sure to locate *Stellar Hermes*. But she had to take the chance, a whole species was depending on her—and so was Hal.

Stellar Hermes darted towards the north pole, Mariska flying as fast as she could manage. She blasted her starship at racing speeds, approaching the surface, and slammed the ship down onto the rocky ground.

Mariska popped her helmet back on, and the two debarked from the space cruiser in a sprint. Hal immediately started palming the ground to feel its structure.

A shriek of happiness erupted upwards from

Mariska's boots: "This is it! The structure feels the same as Minerallia!" Hal walked to the right a few steps and bent down again. He thrust his fist to the ground and the ramp rumbled open.

Mariska's eyes darted around the horizon looking for any signs of space pirates. Thankfully, she saw none.

The two friends ran down the ramp that opened into another underground cavern. The interior of the cavern was a replica of the one on Minerallia, and in the centre was the cylindrical cog they were looking for—completely untouched and intact.

Mariska stood back as Hal climbed onto the console. She didn't know how they were going to get the cog out of here; it was half the height of Hal and probably weighed more than he did.

Hal started feeling around, trying to figure out how to unclamp the cog, when an idea popped into Mariska's head. She called to Hal: "I'm going to get the repulsor-sled, we can use it to get the cog back to my ship—I don't think you'll be able to lift it very far."

"That sounds good. It does look quite heavy."

Mariska reached the top of the ramp and crouched at its edge to confirm they were still alone. She left Hal in the chamber below and she bounded back to her starship. The minimal gravity, and her long legs, made the trip easy.

The airlock and the repulsor-sled weren't compatible:

the sled was too long to fit inside the airlock, so she had to evacuate all the air in *Stellar Hermes* to get the dolly out. Mariska pushed the sled down and out of her ship and towards the stone ramp.

Scanning the horizon again, she made sure there still weren't any pirates in sight. Then she made her way back to the cavern, pushing the floating repulsor-sled in front of her.

Mariska reached the bottom of the ramp just as Hal, groaning, lifted the cog to the ground. Mariska pushed the sled over and Hallvarður toppled the cog onto the repulsor-sled. The sled dipped as it accepted the weight of the cog then slowly rose back to its regular level.

Mariska felt a sting on her leg.

She spun around, and a gang of four space pirates stood menacingly at the bottom of the ramp, pointing blasters at them.

Mariska had been shot. The laser blast had just grazed her leg, but it had punctured her space suit.

Now there were two time constraints: the three quarters of an hour they had left to get back to Minerallia—and the four minutes she had left with air.

Mariska could feel the freezing cold biting at her leg. She needed to get back into the environment of *Stellar Hermes*—and quickly. But there were obstacles in her way.

The space pirates that blocked their exit were a mixture

of humans and aliens, men and women. Some were short and burly, some were tall and sinewy. And they were all formidable.

Mariska made a snap decision: she hurtled the repulsor-sled towards the pirate on the left, knocking him over.

At the same instant Hal dispatched two of the alien pirates on the right with his rock moving powers.

NAN-C darted forward and started to distract the remaining pirate by blasting their face with an electro-shocker, but the burly pirate just knocked NAN-C aside.

Mariska picked up a rock and chucked it at the remaining pirate. The impact was so strong—with the limited gravity—that the pirate was sent flying into the wall, knocking him unconscious.

The space pirate Mariska knocked over with the sled was getting back up. He was a tall, muscle-bound human with a grumpy face, full of scars. He pushed the repulsor-sled aside and lunged at Mariska, knocking her to the ground, pinning her there with his weight.

Mariska wriggled side-to-side and managed to push the pirate off. She jumped to her feet and almost collapsed with the pain that shot through her leg. The pirate stood up, directly in front of her, and brandished his blaster. Mariska froze, not knowing what to do.

But it didn't matter. A large boulder appeared from her side, slammed into the pirate's thick chest, and pinned him on the ground.

Mariska's remaining oxygen was quickly depleting, and the extreme frost bite on her leg was stinging.

Hal took charge, and ran up the ramp first, Mariska following close behind with the repulsor-sled. She knew the pirates they had just finished dealing with were probably just the welcoming committee.

And she was right—

When they crested the top of the ramp, three more pirates were waiting—and three pirate star fighters were perched nearby.

Mariska's only thought was getting aboard her starship. She was gasping for air now and the cold was creeping up her leg.

She took off towards *Stellar Hermes* as fast as she could hobble, but the pain in her leg slowed her down. The frost bite and lack of pressure were turning the exposed skin black.

A laser blast zinged past her head, just missing.

Another dinged off the side of the repulsor-sled.

Hal took a blaster shot in the shoulder, but it didn't slow him down—it was like shooting the ground.

As they reached the landing ramp, Hallvarður stopped and turned around, while Mariska limped up as fast as she could.

Hal knelt on the ground and three separate chunks

of rock burst upwards, launching the three pirates into space.

Mariska was waiting, panicked, at the top of the landing ramp. She couldn't breathe and there was no atmosphere in her ship because she evacuated it to fit the repulsor-sled out.

Hal came trudging up and into *Stellar Hermes* and Mariska slammed the airlock behind him. She keeled over on the floor rasping for breath, waiting for the onboard atmospherics to reach appropriate levels.

There was a ding in her helmet, and slowly, with painful muscles, she unlatched and removed her helmet. She took the deepest breath of her life, and felt the warm oxygen flow into her lungs.

But she didn't have any time to think—

Stellar Hermes jolted with the blast from a turbo laser.

And again—

Mariska, her leg still stinging and throbbing, stumbled into the pilot's seat and started to take off—fortunately she had left *Stellar Hermes* running.

She ignited the deflector shields to help protect against the energy blasts, and launched away from the moon.

But the three pirate star fighters had already launched and were honing in on her vessel with turbo lasers blazing—

Chapter 15

Pursuit of Pirates

Mariska hated space pirates—especially skilled space pirates in fast, sleek, formidable star fighters with turbo lasers.

Her only chance of escape was to evade them in the unpredictable asteroid field. Since *Stellar Hermes* had no offensive capabilities, only the protection of the shields and Mariska's amazing piloting skills would keep them safe.

The starship took a couple more laser blasts to the deflectors, but the shields held steady as they blasted towards the edge of the clearing.

Mariska rolled her ship behind a large asteroid and pitched underneath the next, trying some evasive manoeuvres, hoping to lose one of the trailing fighters. But, of course, the pirates were too good for that.

Another turbo laser blast rocked the hull of *Stellar Hermes*. The two companions bounced in their seats but Mariska remained very focussed and knew that she had to employ some fancy tricks to lose the pursuers.

In front, she noticed two asteroids hurtling towards each other. If she timed it just right she could squeeze between them before they exploded into tiny pieces. Mariska made a few minor adjustments then pushed the lever forward for more thrust.

She angled her ship between the two oncoming asteroids—a slight miscalculation on her part and the two rocks would crush her ship instantly.

Mariska's heart was racing.

Hal, wide-eyed, was clutching his seat tightly.

The asteroids were closing.

She couldn't blink, she needed to see every nanosecond of what was happening.

At the last second she questioned her calculations and rolled *Stellar Hermes* to port—and it was a good thing—

The asteroids had closed further together than she realized. *Stellar Hermes* jolted as one of the asteroids grazed the tip of the ship's thrust vectoring ailerons.

The asteroids exploded in a mess of flying pieces of rock. The ejecta spewed in every direction at a velocity faster than the original asteroids. Bits and pieces knocked against the back of the fleeing *Stellar Hermes*.

One of the larger chunks twirled towards a pirate fighter and slammed into the cockpit window. The window cracked and all the air puffed out. The next instant the pirate ejected, propelled upwards by the seat's rockets, and the enemy pilot floated aimlessly in a spacesuit.

The other two star fighters made it through, dodging and twirling and rolling around the rogue asteroid pieces.

One down, thought Mariska, as she continued flying. The back of her brain reminded her that she was on a schedule, with less than an hour before Minerallia crashed into Mycota.

She was so focussed on the task of piloting her ship that she barely noticed the searing pain in her leg.

Mariska spun her spaceship downwards, evading a twirling ice ball. She tilted her star cruiser to port, hugging next to an almost spherical rock. Each manoeuvre distressing Hal a little more.

The turbo lasers of the pursuing star fighters lanced at her ship, usually missing, or being intercepted by a flying chunk of stone. Some of the shots were direct hits that would rock her starship—but with her upgraded shields they weren't getting through. Some of the shots would spear a space object in front of her, exploding it into smaller pieces, forcing Mariska to react quickly to evade the debris.

Mariska could sense Hal's tension as he sat rigidly beside her—it was only heightening her worry. This game was taking up too much of their valuable time—and the lives of all the Minerallians were in her hands.

Thankfully, one of the pirate star fighter's luck ran out. It exploded into bits in a flash of bright light, after miscalculating the speed of an asteroid and hitting it dead on.

QX, one left. Either the most skilled or the luckiest.

Mariska tried hugging to the curvature of an asteroid, swinging completely around the object and coming out facing the other direction. But the pirate followed.

She tried skimming the surface of a gigantic asteroid, dodging stalagmites like she did in the Mycotan canyon. But the skilled pirate was still on her tail.

She even tried accelerating towards one of the asteroids and pulling up at the very last second. Hal grunted with the abrupt change in direction. But the pirate saw her plan and hung back.

The whole time, the pirate's turbo lasers streaked towards her ship, jolting the star cruiser, grazing its strong shields, or missing completely.

She was starting to get desperate, and she was running out of asteroid field—and time. Maybe she could outrun the pirate in open space.

Mariska gave up on evasive manoeuvres and concentrated on getting out of the asteroid belt quickly and safely. When she had a moment to look down at her console, she plotted the hyperspace route back to Minerallia.

She was going to try jumping to hyperspace metres after clearing the asteroid belt. It was a dangerous manoeuvre because she could risk a backwash that could suck an asteroid into hyperspace with her. External bodies trailing star cruisers in hyperspace was bad news for everybody.

But it was her only chance!

Mariska could see the end of the asteroid mess. She could feel Hal's body tensing. She dodged around an ice ball and just started to clear into open space—

The space pirate blasted a turbo laser and an asteroid to the starboard side burst apart into a smatter of smaller pieces—

It was too late to avoid, Mariska had already punched into hyperspace—along with a few of the smaller rock pieces.

Not only was the desperation of the Minerallians weighing on her, but now there were asteroid chunks alongside her vessel in hyperspace.

They wouldn't cause any problems during the jump,

but on exit they could do anything. They could continue forward at hyper speed and if they connected with a planetoid it would be devastating. They could lurch sideways and blast a hole right through *Stellar Hermes*. Or if everything went well, they would do nothing.

The trip back to Minerallia was tense. Neither of the duo said a word. Mariska was stressed about her ship. Hallvarður was stressed about his people. And they were both really worried they wouldn't get back in time.

Mariska saw on the scanner that two asteroid chunks had followed her wake into the hyper tunnel. She stared at them, willing them to be polite on the other side.

It was time—

Mariska closed her eyes, hoping for a good outcome, and slowly pulled back on the hyperspace control lever—

One of the asteroid pieces accelerated forward at near hyper speeds. It ricocheted off the second piece, sending it careening away from Mycota and Minerallia, but not by much. If the piece had collided with the planet it would have torn the sphere apart.

The second chuck slammed into the side of *Stellar Hermes*, knocking the yoke out of Mariska's hands. The starship spiralled towards Mycota. But Mariska wasn't going to crash on that planet again.

She grabbed the controls and wrenched them to the side, just managing to gain control as they hurtled too close to the planetoids for Mariska's liking.

Directly in front of the ship, Minerallia was burning through the atmosphere, getting critically low.

Mariska sped up her ship and blasted towards the north pole of Minerallia. She was going to have to enter the atmosphere along with the moon and perform a dangerous landing on a fast moving—and extremely hot—object.

Mariska struggled to keep *Stellar Hermes* from crashing as the ship was jerked from side to side by the atmospheric turbulence of the moon.

A chunk of the moon broke off and bolted just past the starboard side, narrowly missing the ship.

Mariska managed to land the vessel on the north pole and the two friends jumped up ready to complete their arduous task.

As Mariska started to walk on her damaged leg, she remembered her space suit was ruptured. She couldn't exit the ship.

Hal would have to do it all by himself.

"Hal, I can't go with you! My suit is wrecked and it's too hot!"

"I understand," responded Hallvarður.

But the problems were even worse. They realized that they couldn't get the repulsor-sled out of *Stellar Hermes* because that would mean opening both hatches to the airlock at once: evacuating all of Mariska's air, and letting in the thousands of degree heat.

"Hal, can you carry the cog by yourself?" asked Mariska.

"I will have to—my people are depending on me!"

Mariska looked into his brave eyes and handed him the ancient key—nothing would work without it.

Hal stood the cog upright in the airlock and closed the inner door. Mariska opened the outer hatch and could feel the rush of heat buffet against the porthole.

Hal rolled the cog down the ramp. As soon as he hit the bottom he started smoking with the extreme heat. *It's a good thing he's made of rock and stone.*

Everywhere around them the searing heat was making the ground glow and *Stellar Hermes* was getting noticeably hotter inside.

Mariska watched through the porthole as Hal rolled the cog down the ramp, into the cavern, and disappeared from her sight.

Mariska stood tensely at the airlock. She hated waiting. She could feel the heat radiating around her. She could feel the moon plummeting to its death.

She waited...

And waited...

Mariska couldn't stand still. She started twisting back and forth, looking out the porthole every couple seconds. If her leg didn't hurt so much she'd be pacing.

Maybe I should have sent NAN-C out after him?

Her heart was racing. Beads of sweat were dripping down her forehead. Her hands were shaking.

I think I have a repair kit for my spacesuit. Maybe I should use it and go help Hal.

Mariska checked out the porthole again: nothing.

What's taking Hal so long?

Finally, after what felt like an eternity, Mariska saw Hallvarður's head reappear from the cavern.

He bolted up the landing ramp and into the airlock. Mariska sealed the outer hatch but did not open the inner one—Hallvarður was too hot.

Hal stood in the airlock, glowing from the heat. Mariska turned on the fire suppression spray in the airlock and left Hal to cool down.

She limped on her painful leg back into the cockpit and immediately launched her ship into space—she didn't want to hang around any longer if this plan didn't work.

She piloted *Stellar Hermes* away from the crashing planetoid to a safe distance where they could both watch.

A minute passed and nothing changed.

Hallvarður, now cool from the fire spray, let himself into *Stellar Hermes* and sat down, watching with Mariska out the front windows.

Another long minute passed—

Minerallia started to break apart—not randomly, but

in a very controlled and structured fashion.

The cog and the key must be working.

The friends sat on the edge of their seats as they saw Minerallia unfold. Two ginormous legs spread out. Two gigantic arms opened up. And a colossal sculpted head sprouted from the massive shoulders—

The moon was an astronomically large Minerallian!

But it was still falling towards the planet, fiery hot.

The protector plummeted towards the surface of Mycota. At the last second it bent its knees to soften the crash. The impact created a huge blast crater, sending dust and particles up into the atmosphere.

Then the protector jumped—

And thrust itself upwards, through Mycota's atmosphere, breaking orbit, and launching into outer space.

The gigantic Minerallian protector moved through space at extremely high speeds, with Mariska and Hallvarður following close behind in *Stellar Hermes*.

It was absolutely enormous, with round chunks of the moon on its arms, legs, head, and torso—just as you would expect if a sphere had unfolded. The newly visible interiors of the moon were gorgeously sculpted of the myriad of rocks, minerals, and gems that exist in the universe.

Mariska and Hallvarður stared out the window in

bewilderment, their mouths agape, as they watched the transformed moon speed through space.

The giant Minerallian was travelling so quickly that it took only a short time for it to reach its destination: the third planet in The Old System. After achieving a stable orbit, the protector gracefully folded itself back together: tucking up its legs, wrapping its arms around, and slowly bending its head down.

Minerallia was a moon again.

The rock-eating Mycotazens were a planet away.

Hal's people were safe.

Mariska finally let out the breath she had been holding.

Epilogue

Mariska was really excited to see her good friend Hal; they hadn't seen each other for over a month.

After they had saved Minerallia, Hallvarður had stayed on the planet to help everyone recover, and Mariska had to get to a hospital station immediately to get her leg treated.

The Minerallians had treated her like a hero. Even though Hal said they didn't want to be saved, they seemed to be happy about it. Mariska didn't like all the attention, but she was very grateful for their appreciation.

They had even gifted her with all the minerals—diamonds and gold—she could carry. Mariska put it to good use. After she was released from the hospital, she took *Stellar Hermes* to the best mechanic she knew, and repaired and upgraded her home into something faster, better, and more efficient.

She even had lots left over to replenish her savings.

But she did miss Hallvarður.

And now she was even aching to get back to work. She had received a call from her pal, Zefram Teeg, with a delivery that sounded dangerous—on the planet Sem.

Mariska was hoping that Hallvarður would come with her.

She landed her star cruiser on the outskirts of a Minerallian city that was being revitalized by the newly reborn rock giants. The planet they were now orbiting was a ball of rock and mineral—everything they needed to rebuild their civilization.

Mariska donned her spacesuit and lankily clambered down the landing ramp of *Stellar Hermes*. Hallvarður was waiting for her at the bottom.

He was big and bulky again, like when Mariska had first met him. He needed the extra arms and strength for the building efforts.

Mariska ran up to Hal. NAN-C bobbed over and clamped onto Hal's bulking, bright red shoulder. Mariska said happily: "Hey, Hal!"

"I'm so happy to see you! I've missed our quiet time together," he responded.

Mariska got a little emotional. Tears started to appear in her eyes, but she wouldn't let it go any further than that.

She looked up at him, and knowing it would sacrifice her precious alone time, asked: "I have a new courier job; would you care for another adventure?"

Acknowledgements

There are so many people who I'd like to thank for supporting me in this endeavour. The person who deserves the most thanks is Liz, my amazing partner-in-crime—without her support and encouragement I wouldn't have started.

My test readers and editors were extremely important to the story's development: Mom, for her love and encouragement; Dad, for someone who doesn't read, actually reading my book; Margaret for editing and support; Jacqui for fantastic editing; and Jane for helping me understand my audience and for her hours of editing.

Finally, I want to express my extreme gratitude to my readers, for opening their imaginations to my corner of the galaxy.

thomasjbradley.ca
hey@thomasjbradley.ca

About the Author

Thomas J Bradley

Thomas loves the infinite possibilities and the endless wonder of space. He is especially fond of distant galaxies with unusual aliens piloting gigantic battling spaceships—with lasers. He distinctly remembers one childhood afternoon when his parents took him to the video store and his Dad pointed to an older movie sitting on a tucked away shelf: *Return of the Jedi*. Thomas's life was transformed as his newly science-fiction–infused imagination blossomed. Thomas believes that the wonder of The Universe can bring excitement and hope to anybody.

Thomas currently lives in Ottawa, Canada, where he spends his days teaching web design and development at Algonquin College and his nights with his wonderful wife, Liz, and their three excitable pups: Paddington, Corduroy, and Wellington. He has previously written two children's stories: *Bartholomew the Bragging Bullfrog* and *High, Low, Over & Under*.